AUTHOR'S NOTE

There are a number of modern royals in India. But for the sake of my story, the royals and their territories that I have used, are all part of my imagination. Please don't go searching for the places. They don't exist. While the places Udaipur, Bhatewar and Khempur exist, the kingdoms, palaces and their citizens do not exist outside my imagination.

Books by Sundari Venkatraman

Standalone novels
The Malhotra Bride
Meghna
The Madras Affair
An Autograph for Anjali
Twin Torment
Finding Anya
Mr. Perfect
Man Friday
Her Prince Charming
Love in Agartha
Arjun's Penance
The Floundering Author
Once Bitten Twice Lucky
Ryan Finds a Bride
Tinder Loving Care
Shaan Gets Hitched
For Better or For Worse
Heartthrob
Call of the Heart
Sing For Me

Collection of shorts
Matches Made in Heaven
Tales of Sunshine

The Groom Series Trilogy
#1 Groomnapped
#2 Gobsmacked
#3 Grounded

Dashavatar (Indian Mythology)
MATSYA: The First Avatar
KURMA: The Second Avatar
VARAHA: The Third Avatar
NARASIMHA: The Fourth Avatar
VAMANA: The Fifth Avatar
PARASHURAMA: The Sixth Avatar

The Writer's Toolkit (Non-fiction)
Publishing Your Book on Amazon
KDP

Marriages Made in India Series
#1 The Runaway Bridegroom
#2 Her Smitten Husband
#3 His Drunken Wife
#4 Her Secret Husband
#5 The Casanova's Wife
#6 Her Bohemian Husband

The Bansal Legacy Trilogy
#1 Simha International
#2 Rose Garden International
#3 Maharaja International

Written in the Stars Series
#1 Scorpio Superstar
#2 Leo's Desire
#3 Taurus Temptation
#4 Virgo's Krush

The Thakore Royals Trilogy
#1 The Marriage Predicament
#2 Tied in Knots
#3 The Wooing of the Shrew

Romantic Shorts
#1 *Chahti Hoon Tumhe*
#2 Beauty is but Skin Deep
#3 Madeinheaven.com
#4 An Arranged Match
#5 The Reluctant Bride
#6 Shweta ka Swayamvar
#7 Papa's Girl
#8 Red Rose Dating Agency
#9 Rahat Mili
#10 Reema's Matchmakers
#11 The Matchmaker's Dream

**The Princess Series
(Historical Romance)**
#1 The Passionate Princess
#2 The Rebel Princess

The MARRIAGE PREDICAMENT

THE THAKORE ROYALS
BOOK 1

A Romance Novel by

SUNDARI VENKATRAMAN

FLAMING SUN

Notion Press Media Pvt Ltd

No. 50, Chettiyar Agaram Main Road,
Vanagaram, Chennai, Tamil Nadu – 600 095

First Published by Flaming Sun 2018
Printed & Distributed by Notion Press
Copyright © Sundari Venkatraman 2023
All Rights Reserved.

ISBN 979-8-88935-982-1

Cover design by: Unaiza Merchant
Edited by: Preeti Arora
Edited & marketed by: The Book Club

DEDICATION

I dedicate this book to the #metoo campaign

ABOUT THE AUTHOR

Sundari Venkatraman is an Indie Author who has 61 books to her credit. These books have consistently featured in the Top 100 Bestseller Lists on Amazon Kindle, in both romance as well as Asian Drama categories. Her latest hot romances have all been on #1 Bestseller slot in Amazon India for over a month.

THE MARRIAGE PREDICAMENT is the first book in The Thakore Royal trilogy; also, the first romance written by the author based on Indian Contemporary Royals. This kindle book remained in #1 Bestseller position on Amazon India for six months in the Contemporary Romance and Asian Drama categories.

Even as a child, Sundari absolutely loved the 'lived happily ever after' syndrome and she grew up on a steady diet of fairy tales, Phantom comics and Mandrake comics. It was always about good triumphing over evil and a happy ending after the protagonists surmounted all unexpected obstacles.

Once she entered her teens, Sundari switched her loyalties from fairy tales to Mills & Boon. While she loved reading both of these, she kept visualising what would have happened if there were similar situations happening in India; to local heroes and heroines. And of course, the joy of vanquishing the ubiquitous evil villains! Her imagination soared and she happily ensconced herself in a rosy romantic cocoon for many years.

Then came the writing—a true bolt from the blue! And Sundari Venkatraman has never looked back.

She walked up to his desk and perched on one corner, not far from him. "Just. I'm done with my work and wanted to check if you needed something done." Yashodhara looked into his warm brown gaze as she spoke to him, feeling colour steal into her cheeks as she noticed the banked heat there. An inadvertent sigh shuddered through her body, startling her in its unexpectedness.

"What was that for?" Indrajeet's dark eyebrow went up in query as it touched his hairline.

Yashodhara clenched her hands into fists as she so itched to run her fingers through his hair. He had no qualms brushing her hair almost every night, just before they went to sleep. But she had never dared to touch him. She was shaken by the strong feeling of temptation, so compelling that she clenched her fists all the harder.

Seeing her discomfort, Indrajeet took the fist closest to him in both his hands and looked deeply into her hazel green eyes. Opening her fingers one by one, he pressed his lips to the palm of her hand, stroking it lightly with a damp tongue.

Yashodhara was surprised to realise that the moaning sound had come from her throat when Indrajeet lifted his head to look up at her. "You said something?" he asked, mischief and desire warring in his eyes.

PROLOGUE

Yashodhara Jadeja stared at her mother, Rani Hyma Devi, her eyes shimmering with tears. "How can I, Mama? You know the situation better than everyone. How can you do this to me?" Her British accent became more pronounced when she got emotional.

Hyma looked at her daughter with both commiseration and adoration in her eyes. Born to her through her first husband, the late Raja Ratansinh Jadeja, Yashodhara was Hyma's only offspring. "You are twenty-four, my child. I can't postpone your marriage forever. We need a man to help us take care of our people, as you have always known. And that was also your father's wish. You are aware this was a stipulation in his will."

Bhatewar used to be a small kingdom before India became a republic. The Jadeja family had ruled the area of five hundred square kilometres, mainly farmlands, since the past four centuries. Raja Ratansinh Jadeja had passed on at a young age, leaving his wife Hyma Devi to take care of their palace and land along with Yashodhara, who was barely two years old at that time.

Raja Ratansinh Jadeja had made his will when Yashodhara had been about thirteen months old. By then, the royal couple had known that they could never have another child. Hyma's womb was too weak to support a second baby. While she had told him that she wouldn't mind him taking another wife, Ratansinh had laughed it off, insisting that Hyma was the love of his life. He had mentioned in his will that his daughter Yashodhara should get married before she became twenty-five and her husband should be made in-charge of the Jadeja land and property.

The Princess of Bhatewar lowered her eyes to the marble floor, failing to come up with a suitable reply. They were royalty, even if only for namesake, in the republic of India. While they had to pay loads of taxes to the government, submitting to its dominion over them, they still had the responsibility of taking care of their 'citizens'. Power came with tremendous responsibility and Hyma Devi took her duties very seriously. She had also drummed that into Yashodhara.

How could she escape from her duty to their people? Yashodhara gave a small nod, refusing to lift her gaze off the floor and look into her mother's eyes.

A deep sigh shuddered from the depths of Hyma's slim frame. She had no solace to offer her daughter. She went about the task of setting up the meeting with the royal Thakore family of Udaipur. The plan was to marry Yashodhara to their eldest born, Indrajeet Thakore. The mother in her never gave up hope that her child would find happiness.

Indrajeet Thakore looked up from his laptop when his grandmother, *Rajmata* Santhini Devi Thakore, stepped into the library. He got up to walk towards her with a wide smile on his face. "Good morning, Grandma. How come you are up and about so early in the morning?" he asked, a gentle, teasing note in his voice as he eyed the clock behind his working chair. It was nine in the morning. While Indrajeet had been up since six, it was rare indeed when the sixty-nine-year-old Santhini Devi woke up before ten.

Santhini Devi pouted at her eldest grandson, the gesture anything but royal. But then, she could be playful when the mood suited her. "Just for you, Indrajeet. This is all about you."

He raised an eyebrow, waiting for her to continue as he helped her on to a newly brocaded sofa. He pulled a velvet pouffe, lifted her feet gently and placed them on the footstool. He settled down next to her and said, "Now tell me, have you had coffee or breakfast?"

Santhini Devi gave a mild shudder, shaking her head. "No breakfast for me. I did have coffee, but wouldn't mind another cup."

Indrajeet went and opened the door to his study and beckoned to the footman hovering around the main hall. "Ramlal, could you please get two cups of coffee?" He didn't notice Santhini Devi wince as he shut the door to go back and sit next to her.

"Indrajeet! This is probably the only thing that I don't like about you. You…"

"What?" There was amusement in his voice as he eyed his grandmother with his coffee brown eyes which were the exact shade as hers.

"That's another thing. Don't you dare interrupt while I'm speaking. Have some respect for the *Rajmata*. You…"

Indrajeet laughed softly, hugging his grandmother. "You *na*, Grandma, have too many conditions. And it looks like you have a number of things you don't like about me."

Santhini Devi gave a dramatic sigh, rolling her eyes towards the ceiling. Her expression immediately changed to one of joy when she eyed the freshly renovated fresco on the high ceiling of the royal library that her grandson had converted into an office-cum-study for himself. "That's alright. I forgive you everything." She looked at her grandson with affection. He reminded her more and more of her long-departed husband. "Just because you have brought our palace back to its former glory. But tell me something, Indrajeet, is it really necessary to go out into the hall and give an order for coffee? Can't you just ring the damn bell? Aren't we royalty?"

Indrajeet guffawed even as he heard a knock on the door. He got up to open the door, and let Ramlal in. The lackey carried a heavy tray which held a silver coffee service with two exquisite bone china cups and saucers, along with a plate of homemade cookies. He took the tray from the other man and dismissed him with a nod of his head before placing it on a low table in front of the *Rajmata*.

"There you go again. What's wrong with you, Indrajeet? Why don't you behave like the prince that you are?" Santhini Devi was totally frustrated.

"Grandma, I've accepted you for the old tyrant you are. Why don't you just accept me for what I am? I don't like standing on formality. Poor Ramlal is older and weaker than me. Now drink the coffee like a good girl before it gets cold," he insisted, pouring the coffee into two cups and handing one to his grandmother after adding milk and sugar to it.

Santhini Devi shook her head at her grandson as she took the cup from him and sipped from it delicately, her little finger held aloft, bringing a smile to Indrajeet's face.

"So, have you been enjoying yourself at the Le Royale Club?" He had paid for the exorbitant membership four years ago, making his grandmother the happiest woman on this planet. She had also begun to adore Indrajeet—a difficult task for the cranky old matriarch who loved only herself—from then on.

"Of course, I've been. What kind of a question is that?" She looked down her nose at him which was no easy task as he topped her by many inches even whilst they were seated next to each other. "Can't you see that I've lost weight and look way younger than before?"

Before becoming a member of the club four years ago, the *Rajmata* had had no purpose in life but to criticise all her family members and whoever was crazy enough to go within ten feet of her. She also used to be extremely overweight. But nowadays, she was happy rubbing shoulders with other members of royalty and also using the gymnasium, swimming pool and beauty salon at the club on a regular basis.

Indrajeet nodded with a smile on his face. "That you do. I'm glad to hear that. So, what's up? What made you wake up so early in the morning?"

She handed her empty cup to him before picking up a cookie and taking a delicate bite from it. "It's about your marriage. There's a wonderful alliance which has come forth. Princess Yashodhara of the Jadeja royal family is the only offspring of Rani Hyma Devi of Bhatewar. Her father, Raja Ratansinh Jadeja, passed away when she was but a baby. She's beautiful and highly educated. In fact, she completed her final years of schooling and degree from England. She'd make you an ideal wife."

Indrajeet shook his head at Santhini Devi, a look of astonishment on his face. "You're joking, right?"

Santhini Devi glared at him. "Sometimes, Indrajeet, you're worse than Rajvardhan. I thought it's only your brother who likes to behave like a joker all the time, while you take life a bit more seriously. Which part of what I said seemed like a joke to you?" Rajvardhan was younger to Indrajeet by two years. The *Rajmata* and Rajvardhan were constantly at loggerheads as he teased her at every opportunity and she didn't take kindly to his treating her like a sibling rather than his grandmother, the *Rajmata* at that. Only he refused to take her seriously.

The more patient Indrajeet replied, "But, Grandma, I'm going to be all of twenty-nine and that too only next month. What's the rush to get married? And I'm not too keen on an arranged match. Let me find my own girl."

Santhini Devi sighed. "Twenty-nine is not young, Indrajeet. You have had almost three decades to find yourself a match. Obviously, you haven't met anyone."

Juliana's face flashed before his mind's eye—her honey blonde hair, violet eyes and pouting lips, neatly packed into a diminutive, but sexy figure—distracting him from the conversation. Indrajeet pulled his mind back to the present with an effort before addressing his grandmother. "That's right; I haven't met anyone that I want as my life partner. But what's the hurry?"

Santhini Devi sighed, eyeing her handsome grandson. "Twenty-nine is a good age to get married. Your grandfather was way younger than you when we tied the knot. Nowadays…"

Indrajeet laughed. "But Grandma, it was different in those days. This is the twenty-first century. I'd rather wait."

Santhini Devi glared at him. "There you go again, interrupting me. Listen, why don't you meet the princess? If you both like each other, we will proceed with the alliance. Otherwise, we can forget the whole thing. Can't you do this much for your grandmother?"

Indrajeet grinned. "Such obvious blackmail, Grandma! Can't we just say no to the alliance?"

His grandmother shook her head at him. "Not this time, no. Let me draw your attention to something, just in case you didn't notice. Bhatewar is our neighbouring kingdom. The Jadejas are our closest royal neighbours. How can we just say no when they have approached us for an alliance between the two families?" She gave him a sly look. Santhini Devi was still extremely unhappy that they had been cornered into selling their summer palace due to financial constraints a few years ago. She was hoping to expand their land and property when this alliance clicked as the Jadejas were both cash rich and still owned vast well-maintained estates. The mother was seriously keen to have a man in charge of their commercial assets. The mother and daughter duo were all that was left of the family.

"So, what's Papa saying about this?" He was careful not to bring his mother into the equation since his grandmother didn't much care for her daughter-in-law's views.

"Why will your dad refuse such an opportunity? He's all for it."

"Really! Then how come he never said anything to me?"

"That's because I insisted on talking to you myself. Listen, Indrajeet, only you and I take any kind of responsibility towards our royal lineage. You father gave up long ago. Otherwise, Gajendar would have never sold our palace to Ritvik Bansal and allowed him to convert it into a five-star hotel." She sniffed loudly. She had never forgiven her son for selling a property which had been in the Thakore royal family for the last few generations. The dominating Santhini Devi didn't have a high opinion of her only son Gajendar and just about tolerated him. She could never empathise with his struggles to hold the land and property together, what with crops failing year after year due to consistent droughts and floods.

But Indrajeet truly admired and respected his father. "Come on, Grandma. Papa was being practical when he took that decision. Today, if I am able to set up a business and handle our farms it's only because of my expensive education as well as the capital back up which papa had set aside. And all that wouldn't have been possible if Papa hadn't sold the palace. We were strapped for cash, Grandma, as you fully well know. Stop talking as if it was all Papa's fault." Indrajeet held back his temper as he spoke softly to the matriarch.

"That's alright. I won't say a word against your mother or father. Forget about them. Now tell me when we can go meet the princess."

"Grandma, I…"

"Why don't you and I go and just meet Yashodhara and her mother? You don't need to give your answer immediately. No one is going to force you to marry any girl that you don't want to." Santhini Devi was insistent.

Indrajeet eyed her stubborn face before giving her a hug. "Determined, aren't you? Have it your way then. Let's go meet your princess."

Santhini Devi gave him a wide smile. "That's my boy." She got up immediately. "Let me go and talk to Rani Hyma Devi and fix a date for the meeting."

"You do that," said her grandson, totally unperturbed.

The Thakore scion was well grounded and happy in his space. If he and Princess Yashodhara liked each other and seemed compatible, maybe they might even consider marriage. He would know this only after he struck up a friendship with her. Right now, he had work to do. Indrajeet mentally shrugged his shoulders as he went back to sit on his office chair, continuing to work on his laptop, putting his grandmother's visit completely out of his mind.

ashodhara gave Ebony his head as rider and horse galloped as one across the Jadeja acres which were lush with wheat and barley crops ripe for harvesting. The colour of the horse's coat and Yashodhara's waist-length hair were the exact same shade of ebony. Except for the white star on his forehead, the horse was completely black. He was also Yashodhara's best buddy for the past two years, from the time she had returned from England, where she had been living for more than the past decade.

Whether in England or in Rajasthan, Yashodhara was always alone. The princess was a loner and had no friends. The only friend she had at school, Chitrangada, the princess of a neighbouring kingdom, lived in the US nowadays. Even before that, they had lost touch when Yashodhara and her mother had moved to England when she had barely been twelve.

Just now, she so wished there was someone she could share her anguish with. A deep sigh shuddered from the depths of her being as Ebony jumped over yet another fence. The horse was in his element, cantering across the fields as Yashodhara had given him his head, not really caring which way he went. Ebony was smart enough to get her back home before his meal time for sure.

She didn't really appreciate the green acres spread around her as Yashodhara was too engrossed with her churning thoughts. The threat of marriage had been looming since the day she had returned to Bhatewar. But she hadn't taken it too seriously until yesterday when her mother had given a name to it, the name of Indrajeet Thakore.

She had checked all about the Thakore prince on the internet and wasn't surprised to find a number of links with his name on them. He was the oldest amongst his siblings and worked diligently to bring the Thakore farmland and palaces to pristine condition. His father, Gajendar Thakore, and his younger brother, Rajvardhan, had supported him whole-heartedly, but it was Indrajeet who had been at the forefront, restoring the royal fortunes.

It seemed as if he had a finger in many pies. He had started off with high-end hostel accommodations for students and office goers who came to Udaipur at some of the buildings on the same premises as their main palace in Udaipur, where they lived. He had started this venture even while he was still studying and working at Harvard.

Later, after he had returned and the palace was restored, most of their heritage properties were thrown open for public viewing at a cost, on all days of the week. Then there were the farms. They had some one-thousand-plus acres of farmland which had been functioning poorly before Indrajeet Thakore had taken over the reins. Nowadays, they were flourishing and populated with happy farmers who reaped a large chunk of the returns. Yes, Indrajeet Thakore seemed to have given back a lot to his people.

There was one more article which mentioned a dilapidated heritage palace that had been restored to its original glory in the village of Khempur. The Thakores had a kind of home away from home in the middle of farmlands. Indrajeet Thakore had had it restored and converted into a showpiece. Rooms were soon to be made available for rent, more like an experience of palatial life. It was mainly foreigners who were expected to stay there. He had had proper roads built throughout the village, connecting to the main highway, and had also got solar panels installed, providing electricity to the whole village. There was also a van that took the village children to the school in the nearest town and brought them back home. The villagers were a much happier lot nowadays.

But all the information didn't make it any easy for Yashodhara to accept that she had to get married. After a point, it didn't really matter who the man was, as long as he helped her run her estate well.

Yashodhara sighed again as Ebony turned his head towards home. Her mother was right. It made sense to tie the knot with the Thakore scion. While the Jadejas had flourishing farmlands too, the younger generation of farmers were up in mutiny most of the time, confident of overpowering the two women as there were no men to back them. And it looked like her father had expected something like this when he made his will two and a half decades ago.

"Bloody MCPs," snarled Yashodhara, close to Ebony's ear as she was bent low over him, spooking the horse. She patted him gently when he reared on his hind legs. "Sorry, my boy, I wasn't talking about you. You are the only man I can tolerate in my life."

Cheering up on that note, Yashodhara entered the tall gates of the Jadeja palace that was home and rode directly to the stables at the back.

"Let me take care of Ebony, my princess," insisted Kishorilal, the head groom, as she jumped down gracefully from Ebony's back.

"Thank you *chacha*," said Yashodhara, giving the groom a wave without looking in his direction. It wasn't exactly shyness which stopped the princess from looking at men directly in their eyes. It didn't really matter whether it was the male servants in the palace or her classmates at school and college in Sussex, it was always the same. Yashodhara just couldn't gather the courage to meet the men's eyes.

She walked into the cool hall of the palace and made her way to the dining room off the kitchen. "Good morning, Mama."

"Good morning, Yasho. Did you have a good ride? I'm so glad to see you back. I just got a call from *Rajmata* Santhini Devi Thakore. The *Rajmata* and her grandson, Prince Indrajeet Thakore, will be coming over for lunch today."

Yashodhara paled as she eyed her mother. "So soon, Mama? You only told me about the matter yesterday." Her hazel green eyes looked accusingly at her mother.

"What's this, Yasho? You'll be twenty-five in eight months. This is the first time you'll be meeting a prospective groom. It may or may not work. Can't you see that we don't have much time? Papa…"

"What will happen if we don't follow Papa's wishes? I know," she raised a palm defensively, "that he meant well. But then, he didn't know what was to happen much later, long after he passed on. Wouldn't you say that the circumstances have kind of changed? Can't I just live my life peacefully without a man in it?"

Hyma Devi sighed heavily. Why had she even believed that it was going to be easy getting her only child married off? "You could do that if we were *aam janta*, common people leading normal lives. But we aren't and you very well know that. We are royalty and have a duty to take care of our people. And we can't do that without a strong male presence here. It's a wonder that we have managed this long. But you did see for yourself when we visited our farms that are situated further away. Some of the younger farmers are even growing banned crops to make quick money. It's next to impossible dealing with these people, and here it's just the two of us. Now, how many times do I need to explain all this to you, Yasho?"

Now it was Yashodhara turn to sigh. "Okay, Mama. Have it your way. So, what's the plan? Do I need to doll myself up for the meeting?"

Hyma Devi laughed, looking at her beautiful daughter. "You don't really need to make an effort is what I think. You already look like a doll. But it would be nice if you wear a sari since the *Rajmata* is visiting."

"Okay." Yashodhara swallowed the breakfast that was served, along with two cups of coffee, not really registering what she popped into her mouth. Her mind was focussed on the afternoon, when she would meet Indrajeet Thakore.

How the hell was she to face him?!

ani Hyma Devi went right up to the main door of her palace to receive her exalted guests even as a footman opened the passenger door to the limousine and helped *Rajmata* Santhini Devi out with a gloved hand.

With a dignified smile on her face, Hyma Devi brought both her hands together in a *namaste* as she greeted Santhini Devi. "Welcome to our humble abode, *Rajmata*. We are truly honoured by your visit."

Santhini Devi nodded her white head royally to the younger woman before turning to look at her grandson as he stepped out of the driver's seat. "Come, Indrajeet. Give me your hand," she commanded regally. No one could make out from her expression that she was thoroughly pissed off by her grandson's clothes. Despite her telling him to change, he was still wearing a pair of designer jeans—that was no consolation to his grandmother—and a white linen half-shirt. Is that how a prince dressed up to meet his bride-to-be and her family? They were also royalty for that matter. His clothes were too casual for the *Rajmata*'s liking. But then, Indrajeet could be so ridiculously obstinate at times.

Hyma Devi stared at the young man who walked towards her to stand next to his grandmother. So, this was Indrajeet Thakore. She had never seen such a handsome man ever before in her life. She decided to ignore his informal attire though it did bother her. His pictures hadn't done him justice. His appearance was definitely princely, what with his height which was obviously well over six feet and his wide shoulders and well-toned arms.

"Sure, Grandma," said Indrajeet as he took the *Rajmata*'s hand before turning around to smile at Hyma Devi.

"This is my eldest grandson, *Kunwar* Indrajeet Thakore. And Indrajeet, meet Rani Hyma Devi of Bhatewar."

"*Namasteji, kaise hai aap?*" Indrajeet shook Hyma Devi's hand firmly.

Hyma Devi gave him a happy nod. "I am fine, thank you. Welcome to our home." She stepped aside and walked along with the grandmother-grandson duo as they entered the wide-open entrance. Walking into the grand hall, she invited them to sit, before calling to a servant to serve some chilled *jal-jeera*, an appetiser typical to North India.

"It's exceptionally hot today, isn't it?" said Hyma Devi, sitting down on a sofa exactly opposite to where the *Rajmata* had settled down with her grandson. Her position also gave Hyma Devi a view of the marble staircase as she waited for her daughter to step down from the first floor.

The two women spoke about the many activities at the club that they both belonged to as Indrajeet looked around silently, his eyes taking in the opulent surroundings. The Jadeja palace was slightly smaller in proportion to the Thakore palace, while it was also done up beautifully with velvet curtains, silk cushions and many artefacts. These were mostly antiques, placed around the main hall in a casual arrangement. Not keen to participate in the conversation, Indrajeet got up to walk to an elephant sculpture that was placed under the stairs as it seemed to call out to him. Made of black granite, it was beautifully carved, with the trunk raised in a salute. It was obviously old and must have probably been in the family for centuries, he thought.

Hearing the gentle sound of anklets, Indrajeet lifted his head to look up at the curving staircase and saw a gorgeous young woman walking down, her steps slow and hesitant. She stopped suddenly, obviously sensing his gaze and looked down at him, her eyes going wide. Even from way down, he could see that she had gone pale as she looked into his eyes, panic in her hazel green ones.

His pulse-rate was steadily shooting up in reaction to her beauty, Indrajeet gave her a smile, realising that she must be Yashodhara. "Hello, princess," he said, his voice soft. He walked to the end of the stairs to wait for her as she still hesitated way above.

Yashodhara felt waves of shock sweeping up her body, making her breathless and faint, as she was unable to take her eyes off the man who had been admiring the granite elephant under the stairs, staring at him in morbid fascination. She immediately recognised him to be Indrajeet Thakore. But none of his photos on the internet had prepared her for the impact of his regal presence. Having consciously kept away from all adult men for almost her entire adult life, the jolt of looking into his chocolate brown eyes was all the more striking for Yashodhara. Beating like a jungle drum, her heart seemed to take a leap into her throat, almost choking her in the process.

It was a few seconds before she realised that he had spoken to her. "Hello," she responded, her voice a whisper. Not having an excuse to continue to remain at the top of the staircase, as far away from him as possible, she walked down the stairs, her hand holding the railing for support as her trembling legs were on the verge of giving out.

Indrajeet couldn't help but stare at the lovely vision who at this minute was walking towards him. Yashodhara was tall and statuesque, regal in her bearing. There may be some who might feel threatened by her build, but not Indrajeet. She appeared perfect to him. Her voluptuous body was draped in a rich printed cream and red chiffon sari, and a matching cream silk sleeveless blouse. Indrajeet saw that slippers of a bold shade of red covered her narrow feet as she took a few more steps down the staircase. She wore a ruby necklace—six strands of them fell down from her neck to her abdomen. They were held together by a circular pendant of diamonds which she was wearing on the left side of her chest.

Her best feature were her eyes, their hazel green converging to a hazel brown closer to the pupils. He watched in fascination as the proportion of green and brown kept shifting with every minute change in her expression, each time she narrowed or widened her eyes. He noticed all this in the few seconds that it took her to walk down the stairs towards him.

"I am Indrajeet Thakore," he introduced himself, taking her hand in his to shake it firmly, a bit startled when he felt the tremor in her hand. He let it go immediately, giving her a questioning look.

"I'm Yashodhara Jadeja." She got the words out with difficulty as her throat felt parched. While she had made the mistake of looking into his eyes when she had been at the top of the stairs—well, she hadn't expected him to be standing at the foot of the stairs— she didn't plan to continue.

Why wouldn't she look at him? Somehow, Indrajeet couldn't believe she was shy. Her body language was anything but timid.

"Shall we?" He offered his arm to her, lifting her hand to place it within the crook of his elbow before walking towards the older women who were waiting for them. He turned to look at her when he felt her hand tremble. "Is something wrong?"

Yashodhara shook her head, looking straight at her mother as she matched her steps with his.

There was no time for any more dialogue between the two before Hyma Devi got up to take her daughter's hand. "Come, Yasho. Meet *Rajmata* Santhini Devi Thakore. And *Rajmata*, this is my only daughter, Yashodhara."

"*Namaste, Rajmata.*" Yashodhara brought her hands together in a traditional greeting as she bowed her head.

"Come, my dear. Sit here beside me," invited Santhini Devi, eyeing Yashodhara keenly, as she patted the space next to her. She had watched Indrajeet guiding the princess towards them and had concluded they looked perfect together.

Yashodhara was relieved to sit with the *Rajmata*. It was any day better than spending more time with Indrajeet Thakore. His touch had made her skin jump and her heart skitter. How she wished that she could be left all alone. Why did her father have to make such a condition in his will and why did her mother insist on following it to the T? She reined in her thoughts when she realised that the *Rajmata* was speaking to her.

"*Haanji!* I finished my BA in Sussex just a couple of years ago. After that, I did a few more courses, all about a few months each, in accounting, administration and managing an estate."

Indrajeet noticed that Yashodhara spoke well with exemplary diction and polished speech. He could see his grandmother nodding in approval. He had to control his amusement when he realised that Santhini Devi was absolutely impressed by Yashodhara's British accent. He bided his time, wondering how to speak with her alone. She looked beautiful, carried herself well, and was educated with good manners. These facts were superficial and simply not enough to decide if they could live the rest of their lives together as man and wife. Though he couldn't deny the frisson of chemistry that he had felt in her proximity, he needed to talk to her, find out what she wanted from life. They would have to know a lot about each other before they decided if they should tie the knot with each other.

Lunch was elaborate, course after course served by a myriad of footmen. After the third course, Indrajeet looked across the table at Hyma Devi and said, "I don't think I can swallow another morsel, Rani Hyma Devi. I am too full." His words were accompanied by a smile that crinkled his eyes.

Hyma Devi looked at him. "But you must taste the *kachori* and *jalebi* that have been specially made for you. Just a little!"

Indrajeet shook his head firmly. "Thank you, but no." He turned to look at Yashodhara who had also pushed her plate away. "If you are also done, princess, could we go for a walk? I need the exercise after the elaborate meal." He got up from his chair, ignoring his grandmother's frown. "You carry on, Grandma, and please excuse us."

Yashodhara got up too, more because she wanted to escape than because she liked the idea of going for a walk with him. "Excuse us, *Rajmata*, Mama," she said softly before walking out of the dining room, Indrajeet at her side.

"I heard that you have some excellent horses in your stable." Indrajeet fell into step beside Yashodhara as they walked out of the front door.

"Yes, some of the best in Rajasthan. Would you like to see them?" She continued to look straight ahead of her instead of at him, even while her reply was polite.

Indrajeet nodded, deliberately not saying anything.

Wondering if he had heard her, Yashodhara turned her head to look at him, her gaze not rising above his chin. When there was no answer forthcoming, she stopped in her tracks. "Shall we go to the stables or would you like to see the gardens?" She continued to address his chin, inadvertently captivated by the cleft on it.

Indrajeet stopped too, not saying anything, willing her to look him in the eyes. He watched in fascination as her eyelashes fluttered before she lifted heavy eyelids to look up at his face and slowly into his eyes. He was startled to see the blood draining out of her face that had gone pale while her eyes shone brightly in the afternoon sunlight. "Is something the matter, princess?" He spoke softly, not keen to startle her as she looked all set to run in the opposite direction. He could sense the tremors emanating from her body.

"Not at all!" Yashodhara shook her head, her eyes on his, unable to hide her fear that was not personal. Why couldn't he tell her if he wanted to see the horses or the garden? Was it such a tough decision? How many times should she ask him? She lowered her eyelids, unable to bear the impact of his brown gaze.

Indrajeet made an effort to shake off the powerful feelings she aroused in him. Looking into her eyes had been like drowning in a turbulent green pool. And what was more, he didn't seem to want to lift himself out. He realised that he was very much attracted to the Jadeja princess. Indrajeet stared at her lips. They were wide and luscious and he was so tempted to press his lips to them. No go! He didn't want to give her a shock. "Let's go see the horses first," he said, relieving her of the task of asking him yet again.

Yashodhara turned left, saying, "This way," as they walked towards the stables at the back of the property. It was a long walk and took them all of ten minutes to reach there. "There are two horses and two mares. This is Bela, my mother's mare. Bela was born right here in this stable and is six years old."

Fond of horses himself, Indrajeet reached out a hand to stroke the mare's forehead. She was brown and white and had a gentle disposition.

They moved on further and met another horse and a mare before reaching the last box. "This is Ebony." There was pride in Yashodhara voice. "He's two years old and belongs to me. He's the best horse in the world." She hugged the horse and nuzzled her face against his neck, startling Indrajeet with the streak of jealousy that he felt at her gesture. It was obvious that Yashodhara and Ebony loved one another.

He reached out a hand to stroke the horse's forehead before rubbing his nose. "Do you go riding often?"

"Every day." Yashodhara kept her face buried in Ebony's neck as she felt safer this way, not having to look at Indrajeet Thakore's face when they conversed.

"What say we go riding tomorrow morning? Oh, by the way, will early morning suit you? I go riding at six or even earlier at times."

Yashodhara jerked away from the horse to stare at him, a startled look on her face. Was he inviting her to go riding with him? But why? She didn't want to spend time alone with him. "I don't understand."

Indrajeet smiled. There was something calling out to him, despite her effort to keep her distance. "Let me rephrase my question. What time do you usually go riding every day?"

With a wary look on her face, Yashodhara replied, "In the mornings, most days. I like to go at dawn. It gives me a chance to watch the sunrise."

"Perfect. I'll see you tomorrow, right here at the stables, at 5.30. Is that fine? Or should I come earlier?"

Yashodhara stared at him, her mouth wide open. "I... I don't know. Should..."

"Listen, Yashodhara. You do know our families are in talks regarding our marriage?" Indrajeet gave her a sharp look, pinning her green gaze with his brown one.

Unable to turn away from his compelling gaze, Yashodhara nodded slowly, feeling breathless as her heartbeats were slowly going crazy. "Yes."

"Well, in that case, you will agree with me when I say that we can't jump into a relationship as strangers, can we?"

She couldn't help noticing how handsome he was. With a broad forehead and thick eyebrows, his eyes were a warm brown, wide set and straightforward. His slashing cheeks ended in a flat clefted chin. But despite all these obvious physical virtues, she still didn't plan to like him. He was, after all, a man. She couldn't stand the species, at least the human kind.

"Yashodhara." Indrajeet called out, his voice rising by a few decibels as he realised she was lost in her own thoughts. "Did you hear what I said?"

Yashodhara eyes went wide as his words registered finally. She nodded again. "That's true."

"That's exactly the reason why we'll go riding tomorrow." Indrajeet turned around to give Ebony a pat before continuing, "Unless you don't want to go with me." He raised a dark eyebrow as he looked at her. "I would rather you went willingly. I'll understand if you don't want to go."

A look of surprise crossed Yashodhara's face. Was he really asking her what she thought about them spending time together? It touched a chord deep within her. No one had bothered to ask her opinion, ever. "I'd like to go." Yashodhara heard herself saying before she could think further.

"Perfect. Let's go back to your palace then. But tell me something, do you people have such an elaborate lunch every day?" He quirked an eyebrow at her yet again.

Catching the amusement in his gaze, Yashodhara burst out laughing, the sound ringing loudly in the cavernous front hall that they had entered, drawing the gaze of Hyma Devi. The princess shook her head at the prince, saying, "That was just to impress you and the *Rajmata*. If we ate at that rate, I'd probably be the size of a giantess by now, wouldn't you say?"

Indrajeet grinned down at her, his warm brown gaze roving over her laughing face, feeling more attracted to her with every moment he spent in her company.

Rani Hyma Devi sighed deeply, happiness stealing into her heavy heart. It had been years since she had heard her daughter laugh wholeheartedly. The Thakore prince was the perfect match for her it seemed.

3

"**J**eet, you went to meet the Jadeja princess today. What do you think?" Ragini Devi asked Indrajeet in a soft voice, eyeing her eldest born with a lot of love.

They had had dinner a while ago and Ragini had been waiting for her mother-in-law, the cantankerous Santhini Devi, to move to her quarters before talking to her son. While the *Rajmata* had spoken about their visit to the Jadeja palace, Ragini wanted to know her son's thoughts on the same.

Shrugging his wide shoulders, Indrajeet took his eyes off the TV sports channel that he had been watching along with Gajendar and replied to his mother. "It's too early to say anything, Mama. Princess Yashodhara is beautiful and it's obvious she's well educated too. But it's too soon to make *shaadi* plans. I am going riding with her tomorrow morning. I'll let you know after we have met a few times and know each other a bit better." He smiled at his mother, giving her a hug. "Are you worried?"

Ragini shook her head. "Not worried, exactly. But a bit anxious, yes."

"About what?" Gajendar joined the conversation.

"I think Mama's worried that Grandma will bring me a wife who's as rude as she is." Indrajeet winked at his father.

Ragini grimaced at the truth her son had revealed in jest. Indrajeet had hit the nail on its head. Not being very outspoken, Ragini was heckled at by the *Rajmata* whenever possible. The old lady walked all over her son and his wife at every opportunity which seemed to be very often. Now Ragini said, "Well, it did cross my mind."

Indrajeet grinned at his mother. "You know me better than that, Mama. I wouldn't marry Yashodhara if she is anything like Grandma. Respecting people is the foremost quality I'd look for in my future wife. And it's also the reason why I want to get to know her better. Let this week go by, and we'll organise a meeting between you two and the Jadejas. What say?"

Ragini frowned. "Only if you're certain. You know how the *Rajmata* doesn't like anyone interfering in her activities. I don't want to bring her wrath on my head."

"Come on, Mama. You and Papa are the most important people in my life. I want you guys to meet Yashodhara and tell me what you think. And I seriously don't give a damn if Grandma doesn't approve. She doesn't own me."

Gajendar laughed, hugging his son. "Spoken like Prince Indrajeet Thakore. I'm proud of you, my son. And yes, I'm keen to meet Princess Yashodhara and Rani Hyma Devi before you take your final decision."

"Done, I'll see how it goes. And there's no need to bring Grandma into the picture." Indrajeet was firm in his views.

Ragini gave a sigh of relief as she leaned her head against her son's wide shoulder, praying for his happiness.

Rani Hyma Devi came wide awake suddenly in the middle of the night, her eyes seeking her bedside clock. It was 2.30 am. Wondering what had disturbed her, she got up to step out of her bedroom and turned right, towards her daughter's bedroom. Walking swiftly, she pushed opened the door noiselessly to check on her daughter as if she were still a child.

"Yasho?" Hyma Devi was startled to see the younger woman sitting on the window sill, looking out of the window.

"Mama? What are you doing here?" Yashodhara turned around to give her mother a startled look from her vantage point. "Why aren't you asleep?"

"I was going to ask you the same question. What are you doing, sitting at the window at this hour? Why aren't you dreaming of your future husband?" Hyma Devi walked further into the room, to go sit next to her daughter on the window sill.

"Tch. You know why, Mama." Yashodhara gave her mother a deep look before turning back to her star gazing, as if she expected to get her answer from the skies.

"Yasho." Hyma Devi patted her daughter's shoulder. "It takes time, you know, to get used to someone new in your life. But it will get better, by and by. Like your father and I, we were strangers when we got married. It took us more than a year to get used to each other." She sighed, thinking of the cruel fate which had taken her dearest husband away from her after less than five years of marriage. "But it was absolutely worth the effort. We had a wonderful life together. You…"

"But, Mama. You know what I'm thinking. It has nothing to do with Indrajeet Thakore. It's me. I don't want to have anything to do with any man. Can't I just be, Mama? I have a good education. I can manage our estate along with you. Then there's *Munshi* Kilachand. He knows A to Zee about everything. Why should I get married?" Yashodhara's face was contorted with anguish as she appealed to her mother.

Rani Hyma Devi sighed, shaking her head vigorously. "Two things, Yasho. One is the stipulation in your father's will. Another is that you know only too well that you are never going to be ready to face the farmers, since they are all men. And I'm not going to be there forever. We…"

"Tch." Yashodhara turned away from her mother to get back to her stargazing, realising the futility of fighting her destiny. It looked like she didn't really have a choice but to marry someone. Did it really matter if it was the Thakore scion or someone else?

"Go to sleep, Yasho." Hyma Devi got up to place a persuasive hand on her daughter's shoulder. "Things are always better after a good night's sleep."

Yashodhara nodded, without turning to look at her mother, willing her to go away and leave her alone to her morbid thoughts. It was all very well for her mother to say that she would feel better after sleeping well. How the hell did one command sleep to come at will?

The Princess sat at the window; her eyes wide open till she saw the stars fade and a flush of orange bathe the skyline with dawn. She got up slowly. It was time to get ready for her early morning date with Indrajeet Thakore.

They met every morning for the next two weeks, enjoying their ride as they checked out the countryside. They didn't speak much, just getting used to each other's company.

On that particular morning, Indrajeet turned Copperhead—his chestnut horse—in the direction of the Thakore palace. "I'd like to invite you for breakfast at my home, Yashodhara." He stopped his horse, reaching out to hold her reins as he spoke to her.

Yashodhara turned to look at Indrajeet. In the past two weeks, there had been some instances when she had forgotten that he was a man and had felt comfortable in his company. He didn't speak much, but created comforting silences which enveloped them as they rode. And she didn't feel threatened by him! Not at all! Maybe, just maybe, her mother had made the right choice for her husband. Yashodhara could even meet his coffee brown gaze a few seconds at a time, without feeling the urge to run away in the opposite direction. And when she made a strong effort to squash her fears, she could even feel the warmth in them. Just now, she stared at Indrajeet with a look of enquiry, not putting her question into words.

Indrajeet smiled as he looked into her hazel green eyes, the morning sunlight bringing out the brown highlights in them. "It's time for you to meet my parents. What say?"

She nodded, realising it had to happen sometime. And anyway, meeting Indrajeet's mother shouldn't be too difficult. She was, after all, a woman, and couldn't disturb her at all.

It was almost eight when they reached the Thakore palace, jumping off their horses before handing over the reins to the groom.

"Welcome to the Thakore palace, Princess Yashodhara."

"Thank you." Her voice was a whisper as she walked through the wide entrance of the massive palace, her trembling hand in Indrajeet's gentle hold.

"Papa," Indrajeet called out to Raja Gajendar Thakore, "see who's come."

Gajendar got up from where he was seated on a sofa in the main hall. "Welcome to our home, Princess." He held out both his hands in greeting as he looked at the beautiful woman standing next to his eldest born.

Yashodhara hesitated before placing her hands in Gajendar's, her eyes looking down. "Thank you, uncle."

Ragini rushed out from the kitchen where she had been discussing the day's menu with the head cook. With a wide smile on her face, she came forward to be introduced to the Jadeja princess. "Welcome to our home, Yashodhara." She hugged the younger woman, reaching up to press a soft kiss on her forehead.

Yashodhara smiled at Rani Ragini Devi, feeling totally comfortable with Indrajeet's mother. "Hello, Aunty. Lovely meeting you!"

"You must be cold. Sit down, I'll get someone to bring you tea. Or do you prefer coffee?" Ragini asked solicitously.

"You sit down, Mama, and talk to Yashodhara. I'll see to the coffee. And get Ramlal to set the table for breakfast."

Ragini gladly sat next to Yashodhara and the two women chatted as if they had known each other for years, while Gajendar watched on, a mellow smile on his face. He liked the princess his mother had chosen for Indrajeet's bride.

Ragini, for one, was glad that her mother-in-law woke up late as the four of them sat down to a breakfast of *poori* and *aloo gravy* along with *pyaaz ki kachori* accompanied by a choice of chutneys. Yashodhara tucked into her breakfast heartily, feeling her appetite return after two weeks. She had lost it since the day

Indrajeet Thakore had visited her home along with his grandmother.

Today, after meeting his parents, Yashodhara realised that while she didn't have a choice but to get married, whether to Indrajeet or someone else, she also arrived at the conclusion that she would rather be a part of the affectionate Thakore family. Both his parents were so nice. And, as for Indrajeet, she had no cause for complaint.

"Are you game for riding back home or would you rather I dropped you by car?" Indrajeet asked Yashodhara as they stepped out of his home after she had said her 'goodbye' to his parents.

"I'd prefer to go by car. Though I'd like to go check on Ebony first."

"Sure. Come along." He led her to the stables which housed a dozen horses and mares. Yashodhara was keen to look around as he introduced her to his horses before they reached a stall where Ebony was standing, looking well fed and content as he swatted his tail lazily at the flies.

Yashodhara walked to her horse and hugged his neck. "I'll come back soon to get you, sweetheart." She patted him gently before turning to Indrajeet. "I'm ready to go."

Indrajeet walked with her to the garage and helped her into the white, low-slung BMW. "She looks beautiful," cooed Yashodhara as she admired the sleek vehicle before getting into the passenger seat.

"Would you like to drive?" Indrajeet offered her the key.

"I'd love to." Yashodhara jumped out of the car enthusiastically before jogging around the bonnet to the driver's side, making Indrajeet smile. This was the second time he had noticed her being so excited about something. The first time was about her horse and now the car.

He settled down in the passenger's seat and wore his seatbelt as she gunned the engine.

"She purrs so smoothly." Yashodhara grinned at him as she reversed out of the garage.

Indrajeet grinned. "Doesn't she?! She's yours if you like her so much." He took a cue from her and gave his car a gender too.

Yashodhara squealed in delight as she braked the car suddenly. "You don't mean that, do you?" She turned to look at him, her eyes glowing with joy.

Indrajeet laughed. If he had done his home-work right, the Jadejas could afford to buy a hundred cars like this without leaving a dent in their bank accounts. But it was her child-like enthusiasm that touched his heart, deep down.

"Why would I say it if I didn't mean it? The car's yours for ever. I'm only happy she's still in mint condition as I had her delivered only last month."

She raised a hand to touch his shoulder. "Thank you."

"The name's Jeet," he said, an encouraging smile on his face.

"Thank you, Jeet. And you can call me Yasho."

"So, what say Yasho? Shall we get married?"

The colour drained from her face even as her smile disappeared. She looked at him warily, her eyes on his, her throat choking. "Are you sure about it?"

"As sure as I can ever be, I suppose. I like you and I find you extremely attractive." He shrugged. "I think we can have a good life together if we work on it."

She liked him and thought he was attractive too. But did that mean they could have a good life together? There were so many things he didn't know about her. And she couldn't talk about them to him. Yashodhara sighed, her shoulders drooping. Why was life such a bitch?!

"What's it, Yasho?" He placed a gentle hand against her shoulder. "You aren't keen on the idea? You can tell me if you don't like me."

She looked at him again, a pathetic look on her face as she shook her head. "I like you, Jeet. That's not the problem. I…"

He grinned, throwing an arm around her shoulders to hug her. "Then let's get married. We'll make it work."

Yashodhara controlled her body from squirming as he pulled her close to his. No, he didn't deserve to be treated like that. Indrajeet had only shown her affection and friendship. She couldn't get someone better than him. That much she knew for sure. That was the moment when Yashodhara decided to take the plunge. "Yes."

Yashodhara Jadeja and Indrajeet Thakore were married a month later in a grand ceremony on the lawns of the Jadeja palace. There were more than a thousand guests who attended the ceremony followed by an elaborate and sumptuous lunch.

Over the past few weeks, Indrajeet had realised Yashodhara wasn't the shy type. But there was something stopping her from being totally spontaneous. Right from the beginning he desperately desired her as his life partner. He admired her spirit and revered her beauty. He wasn't really fazed when she refused to let him touch her. There were times when he held her hand, but that was it. The only time he had thrown his arm around her shoulders, he could feel her tremble. But that didn't worry him too much as they had become friends of sorts. They shared a passion for their land and wanted to help their farmers prosper. They both loved to go on long rides, racing across the flatlands. While this activity didn't really aid talking, they enjoyed each other's company.

As for Yashodhara, she had realised from day one she didn't have a choice but to get married. She sensed that Indrajeet was a gentleman. He was not just good-looking, but chivalrous too. He never stepped into her space, respecting her wish when she made it amply clear with her body language. She admired the way he handled his people, especially the farmers, with respect. While guiding them with a strong hand, he also granted them autonomy.

While she didn't know any man to compare him with, Yashodhara still felt that Indrajeet was the best she could find in a husband. The rest of it she left to fate. As the princess of Bhatewar, she didn't really have a choice but to marry. It was a good thing that their estates were close to each other, even sharing a common fence at the furthest point.

Indrajeet handed his bride into the passenger seat of his black Lamborghini—he had bought it only the earlier week after gifting his BMW to his betrothed—and walked around the bonnet to get into the driver's seat. Loud clapping and catcalls followed them as he drove the car down the long drive of the Jadeja palace and stepped on the accelerator once they left the gates behind.

"I like your choice of cars." Yashodhara complimented her new husband, a small smile on her face, as she tried hard to hide her nervousness.

"I'm glad you like it. You can take it for a spin any time you want to. And so, Mrs Thakore, are you ready for the life of a married princess?" Indrajeet smiled, giving her a sideways glance.

There was no answering smile on Yashodhara's face when she replied, "Is anyone ever ready for that?"

He turned his head to look at her curiously, wondering if she had had some kind of a bitter experience. It was time that they got to know each other well. He was taking her away to his heritage property at Khempur which had been recently renovated—Iravat Heritage Inn. The plan was to rent out the rooms on long term basis to foreigners who wanted to spend a few weeks touring Udaipur and the rest of Rajasthan. Even a couple of TV channels had approached him for hiring the property for shooting. But just now it remained empty, with only a few servants and a cook who resided in a couple of cottages in the same compound.

After an hour's drive, they reached the gates of the Irawat Heritage Inn by twilight. The silence was blissful. Parking the car, Indrajeet got out to walk to the passenger side to open the door for Yashodhara.

She got out hesitantly, refusing to look at his face. She turned instead to gaze at the heritage structure and whistled softly. "This looks beautiful," she said, a wide smile on her face. While she had read about the property on the internet, there hadn't been any pictures.

But no picture could have done justice to what was in front of their eyes. It was a three-storied structure set in the middle of a lush garden full of trees and flowering shrubs. Except for the tarred road for vehicles, the rest of the area was covered in grass.

"Come." Indrajeet took her hand in his as they walked towards the building.

Yashodhara hesitated, instinctively trying to pull her hand out of his. But that was only for a few seconds. His hold was loose, allowing her to decide what she wanted to do. And that was what gave her the confidence to leave her hand curled up in his.

A manservant rushed out to open the main door even before they rang the bell. "*Namaste* Rajkumar Indrajeet aur Rajkumari Yashodhara." Satyapal's body was bent almost double, his hands folded in front of his chest, as he greeted the young master and his bride.

"Hello Satyapal. How are you?" When Satyapal nodded his pepper and salt head vigorously with a wide smile on his face, Indrajeet continued, "And your wife Sita? Her health is good?"

"*Aap ki dua se sab theek hai,* Rajkumarji." The servant guided them to the intricately carved wooden swing that hung from a stand in the middle of the open courtyard, gesturing for them to sit. "Sita," he called out to his wife, "*aarati lekar aavo.*"

A middle-aged woman stepped out from the direction of the kitchen, carrying a silver tray. A *diya* glowed in the centre of the tray. Her face was almost entirely covered with her sari *pallu.* She welcomed the royal couple warmly before rotating the tray in front of them three times in the clockwise direction and three times anti-clockwise, muttering something unintelligible. This was to ward off the evil eye.

Indrajeet sat through the whole procedure with a smile on his face, continuing to hold his bride's hand. He turned to see that she had also pulled her sari *pallu* halfway down her face, refusing to look at anyone in the eyes. He planned to get to the bottom of the matter first thing when he had her to himself.

"Satyapal, can you arrange for some tea for us? We'll freshen up and be right back in a few minutes. Come along, Yash. Let me show you the rooms. You can choose any room you like and we'll stay there. We can even stay in a different room each night if that's what you'd like to do." He gave her a mischievous grin, his eyes crinkling at the corners.

Yes, Yashodhara could see his face despite the transparent chiffon sari covering the top half of her face. And what's with calling her 'Yash'? Who had told her husband that he could call her by that name? She tried her best to be angry with him but couldn't help liking it. Yash in Sanskrit meant success, splendour, majesty and luxury. Why would someone dislike being called by such a name?! It was also short and sweet. With a mental shrug, Yashodhara walked along with her new husband as he took her on a brief tour of the ground floor.

There were three bedrooms on the left and another three on the right side of the courtyard. They walked into a sitting room from where doors opened into the bedrooms. Each had its own en suite bathroom which was huge, bigger than those at her palace back home.

Each room had a different colour scheme. Yashodhara fell in love with the one decorated in yellow and it also had a view of the back garden. She could even see the stables far behind. "You have horses here?" She asked, turning to look at Indrajeet who was supervising the luggage being brought in and placed on a low table next to the carved wooden wardrobe in one corner.

"Yeah, I do. Just two of them. I'll probably add more once guests start arriving and there's a demand for horse riding."

She nodded, her eyes wary as she noticed that two sets of luggage, hers as well as his, had been brought into the room. A huge sigh broke out from within her. Once again, it seemed she had no choice.

"You go on and freshen up. Someone will do the unpacking. I'll wait for you in the courtyard," said Indrajeet, patting her cheek lightly before stepping out of the room, shutting the door gently behind him.

Yashodhara stood where he had left her, holding a hand to the cheek which he had just patted, a stunned expression on her face. She searched her mind for the fear, revulsion, anger and frustration that usually surfaced when any man came within ten feet of her. But there was none. There had been nothing threatening in Indrajeet's touch as he had tapped her on her cheek.

Was there hope for her yet?!

Yashodhara joined Indrajeet ten minutes later, taking a deep breath as the smell of jasmine filled the air. The tiny white flowers winked from their creepers which climbed the compound wall surrounding the courtyard. They had opened up with the advent of darkness and permeated the air with their rich aroma as a gentle breeze blew across the courtyard. She went and sat on the swing that Indrajeet gently pushed with his large, bare feet, and accepted the cup of tea that Sita handed her.

He looked sideways at his new wife, a look of admiration on his face. She wore a long cotton Kalamkari printed skirt in multiple shades of black, red and yellow. The skirt which ended a few inches above her ankles was teamed with a black sleeveless top. *She looks good enough to eat,* he thought as he sipped his tea.

"Would you like to go for a walk around the garden before it gets too dark?" asked Indrajeet, taking the empty cup from her and placing it on a table by the side.

"Yes, please." Yashodhara got up from the swing, keen to have a look around. More than anything, she was worried about the time when the two of them would be left completely alone.

Indrajeet slid his feet into a pair of leather moccasins that he had left on one side, before taking her hand in his. "Do you feel cold, Yash?"

She shook her head. "Not at all, I love the cold weather."

He smiled. So did he! They didn't talk much as they walked in a circle around the garden, Indrajeet pointing out the small temple which was built in a corner. "It's of Lord Krishna." There were two clay oil lamps burning brightly in the small apertures built into the side pillars of the sanctum, while there were two brass lamps hanging from the ceiling on both sides of the deity. These were also lit, throwing light on the marble statue of Lord Krishna, his legs crossed as he leaned against a cow, playing on his flute.

Yashodhara shut her eyes, pressing her hands together as she prayed hard. She prayed for courage and begged the lord to take away her fear, the fear that permeated her heart every second when she got time to think. No wonder she did her best to keep busy.

Indrajeet stared at his wife, instead of the deity he had seen hundreds of times. There was sweat on her brow and her upper lip, despite the chilly weather, while her lashes fluttered restlessly, her fingers locked together, her body taut with tension.

"Yash!" He placed a gentle hand on her shoulder.

Startled, Yashodhara jerked around, her eyes opening in a flash, panic invading her. "Jeet, I…" She choked, unable to go on.

He smiled as he spoke to her. "Is something upsetting you? Do you want to talk about it?"

Yashodhara looked up into his gentle brown eyes, the panic in her hazel green ones receding slowly as she shook her head. "No, nothing!"

He tilted his head to one side, accepting her words for the time being, even though he didn't believe them. "Have you finished praying?" When she nodded, he said, "Then let's go."

They walked for another half an hour. "Let's go riding in the morning. You can see the solar panels that I've had built. All the cottages in the village have been renovated too, with toilets within the premises." There was pride in Indrajeet's voice as he spoke to her about his pet project.

Of course, she would love to see everything, *if* she survived the night that is. Yashodhara could feel her nerves tightening as the witching hour approached.

They had dinner in the dining room off the kitchen which was at the back of the property. There were tables for two, four and six, enough for fifty people to dine at one go. There was only one table set for two that night. Indrajeet led her to it and sat her down before lighting the candles that had been placed in two small glass fish bowls on the two sides.

Their dinner consisted of *chicken soup*, steaming *rotis* with *aloo gobhi* and *Rajasthani laal maas*. While there was *mutton biryani* and *raita*, both of them opted to have only the *raita* before washing down the meal with tall glasses of *masala chaas*.

"Looks like that calls for another long walk," said Indrajeet, laughter in his voice.

Yashodhara couldn't help the grin which broke out on her face despite her nervousness. She patted her stomach, saying, "You're right. Let's go for it."

They stepped into the garden again, walking along the road leading outside the property. The road was well lit and Yashodhara noticed the neatly painted cottages with lights winking in their verandas. She could hear music and dialogues and it was obvious the people living in those houses were watching TV.

On their way back, Indrajeet stopped under a *gulmohar* tree which was not far from the entrance to his property. Leaning against it, he gently pulled Yashodhara in the circle of his arms. "Yash…" He pressed his lips to the top of her head, his arms loosely circling her waist.

Yashodhara squirmed, trying hard to retain some space between their bodies. It wasn't easy. She could feel his lips on the top of her head, making her whole body go warm. But… but… she wasn't comfortable in his hold. She pulled out of his arms and said, "Shall we go? I feel tired. You must agree, it's been a long day." Her voice was small as she looked down at the ground.

"Yash? Don't you like it if I touch you?" Indrajeet asked her outright, rubbing his hands against his arms that felt empty now that he had removed them from around her waist.

What could she tell him? That she wished to be held close in his arms but was terribly scared of her own reaction? And it wasn't as if he would stop at just holding her. He would want more, way more than what she was prepared to give. The blood drained out of Yashodhara's face. She would never be ready for this… this physical intimacy with a man. But then, Indrajeet was not any man. He was her husband. She had promised to be his wife in all ways, that very

morning, when they tied the knot as man and wife. "I...
I..." Yashodhara shook her head, at a loss for words.

"Let's go," said Indrajeet, his hands tucked in the
pockets of his jeans, as he turned to walk towards
the gates of his property, after making sure she was
walking along beside him.

Yashodhara missed holding his hand, his warmth,
the feeling of safety that she had come to look forward
to in his company. But she didn't have the guts to take
his hand right at that moment as they walked back. It
sure promised to be a long night.

"You go on in and get ready for bed. I'll join you
soon," said Indrajeet, leaving her at the entrance to the
bedroom they were about to start sharing.

Yashodhara nodded, not uttering a word as she
watched him go. She felt dejected and wanted to call
him back. But no, what if he demanded more than she
was prepared to give? Actually speaking, what could
Yashodhara possibly offer him?

Why the hell had she let her mother persuade her
to get married?

Indrajeet sat on the swing, pushing it back and
forth with his feet. The servants had left and he
had shut the main door, waiting for his wife to get
comfortable before joining her in their room. Will she
let him make love to her? Somehow, Indrajeet didn't
think so. He could see that she was scared of being
touched, though she didn't object to holding hands.

Well, he was in no hurry. They had their whole
lives in front of them. It promised to be fun, wooing

his wife. It wasn't as if Yashodhara was a cold creature. He had seen her passion for things. She loved food, she enjoyed wearing vibrant clothes. She loved her horse Ebony. She had even fallen for his BMW. She was passionate about helping her people. So, that wasn't the issue. He would win her over. Indrajeet was quite confident of that. With a smile on his face, he got off the swing to walk towards their room.

Knocking gently on the door, Indrajeet entered the bedroom after he heard Yashodhara asking him to 'come in'.

"Hey!" he greeted her as she sat in front of the mirror, running a brush through her black hair which fell below her waist. "Would you like me to do that for you?" Not waiting for her answer, Indrajeet took the silver brush from her nerveless hand and began to brush her hair in long and gentle strokes. He gave her a smile when their eyes met in the mirror. "You must be doing this every night," he asked gently.

"Yes." The word choked in her throat which was feeling extremely dry. What would he do next?

After brushing her hair in rhythmic strokes for all of fifteen minutes, Indrajeet placed the brush on the dressing table before pushing the length of her hair to her left shoulder as he bent down to press his lips to the side of her exposed neck.

Yashodhara shut her eyes, biting down hard on her lips, doing her best to hold back the scream roiling up from the depths of her stomach.

Unaware of his wife's reaction to his caress, except for a slight stiffening of her body, Indrajeet breathed in deeply of her scent, his tongue peeping out to gently stroke the rapidly beating pulse at her neck. Of its own volition, his right hand slid down to cup her right breast.

Indrajeet jumped back in shock when Yashodhara screamed, the sound echoing in the large room, the sound amplified multiple times as it ricocheted off the walls. He just about managed to catch his bride as she fell down from her chair in a dead faint.

5

I ndrajeet lifted Yashodhara's supine body and placed her gently on the bed. Taking a cold towel from the fridge, he sprayed a few drops of *eau de cologne* on it and gently wiped her face and neck with it, glad to see her stirring.

Stroking a gentle hand over her head, he watched her eyes open, a look of panic in them. "Relax, Yash. There's no need to panic. I won't touch you if you don't want me to." He went to get a bottle of water and unscrewing the lid, held it to her lips. "Drink some; it will help you feel better."

Yashodhara got up to sit against the bedhead before taking the water bottle from him. She drank a few gulps of water, willing the dryness in her throat to go away. "I'm sorry, Jeet," she said in a whisper, giving him a pathetic look.

"Forget it. Tell me something. Do you have trouble sleeping?" he asked, out of the blue.

Not expecting the question, she gave him a hesitant nod, saying, "Yes," without thinking. Realising what she had admitted to, Yashodhara bent down her head, unable to face him.

Indrajeet wasn't really surprised by her answer. "Well, let's go to sleep then. I feel beat."

Yashodhara raised her head to give him a surprised look. Somehow it felt as if there were two different lines of conversation happening between the two of them. Why had he asked her if she had trouble sleeping? And why did he ignore her honest reply?

She knew that her husband must be deeply disappointed in her. Would he want to divorce her? Panic filled Yashodhara's stomach as it clenched.

While she sat there in a state of trepidation, Indrajeet took some clothes from his suitcase and walked into the bathroom. He came out a few minutes later, clad in a pair of boxers and a t-shirt. Yashodhara averted her eyes when she noticed that his bare legs were liberally coated with dark hair, her heart beating hard. What now?

Indrajeet went and sat on the other side of the bed, switching off the lights, leaving a small night light on. He lay back on the pillows and said, "Would you like me to hold you? I promise not to do anything but just hold you in my arms. Maybe you'll feel safer and sleep better." He looked at her with his steady brown gaze. "It's entirely up to you. Feel free to come into my arms when you want to." He shut his eyes, breathing slowly and steadily, leaving the decision to her.

Yashodhara stared at her husband in the soft light of the night-lamp, the panic receding completely from her system as she watched the even rise and fall of his chest. He had asked nothing of her, absolutely nothing. He hadn't even got angry because she had screamed and fainted. And at the end of it all, he was ready to hold her in his arms so that she could sleep better. A tear ran down her cheek, soon to be followed by another as Yashodhara sniffled. Not wanting to disturb him, she buried her face in her hands and cried noiselessly, hating herself.

Indrajeet hadn't gone to sleep. He opened his eyes when he heard her sniffles, letting her cry for some time, accepting that she needed the release. After a few minutes, he turned on his back, opening his arms wide, calling to her, "Yash…"

Yashodhara turned around to see her husband's arms open in invitation. Without thinking any further, she fell into them, burying her face in his wide chest, her body still shuddering with sobs.

"No, my sweetheart, there's no need to cry," whispered Indrajeet as he stroked her back gently, holding her close.

Yashodhara turned her head to the side and pressed it close to his heart, his steady heartbeat gradually calming her down. Soon, she fell into a deep sleep, the kind she hadn't experienced over the past so many years.

Feeling her body relax in sleep, her breathing having gone steady, Indrajeet shut his eyes and waited for sleep to overcome him.

The woman in his arms—his wife of a few hours—felt nothing short of delicious. But she was obviously scared of being touched intimately. He had seen the wariness lurking in her eyes whenever he got within a few inches of her. She had let him hold her hand and no more than that.

Was that fear for all men or him in particular? Indrajeet's eyebrows met in a scowl as he wondered about it. Somehow, he didn't think it was personal. If that had been the case, she wouldn't have gone to sleep in his arms just now.

Had she been through some kind of a bad experience? He thought back from the day he met her for the first time. Yashodhara had appeared confident when she spoke to his grandmother. Generally, people tended to get rattled in the presence of the matriarch. But Yashodhara had remained unfazed.

Later, when she had met his parents and siblings, Yashodhara had got along with his mother Ragini Devi and sister Dayanita like a house on fire. But— Indrajeet's scowl deepened—she had kept her head bowed down low when she greeted his father Gajendar, answering him in monosyllables.

Then, when she met his brother Rajvardhan, she had barely uttered two or three words. His brother tended to chat up women too comfortably. But he had just been unable to draw Yashodhara out. Indrajeet remembered feeling happy at that point—that his bride-to-be preferred his company to his flirtatious brother's as many women tended to do.

But it looked like there might be a deeper reason for this sorry episode. The fear he had seen in her eyes, when Yashodhara had screamed a while back, bordered on terror. And to make matters worse, she had fainted.

Indrajeet sighed, his hand gently running through the dark locks of hair spread down Yashodhara's back, as she continued to sleep in his arms, her breathing even. She was enchanting, all woman. But she obviously held some kind of deep pain within. He needed to get to the bottom of it. And for that, he had to earn her confidence. He had, of course, gained her trust to some extent. She wouldn't be sleeping in his arms otherwise. But that wasn't enough for her to accept him as her husband in all ways.

It was going to be a lot of work. But work had never bothered Indrajeet before and he refused to let it bother him now. He had fallen for his wife in a big way and planned to make her his, completely, however long it took him.

With this dreamy thought firmly entrenched in his mind, the scowl disappeared from Indrajeet's face as he sank into a slumber, holding Yashodhara close to his heart.

The next four days, the couple spent chatting about everything under the sun—books, films, horse-riding, travelling, managing their estates and more. Indrajeet kept watching her for signs that would show him that she was ready for a personal dialogue.

Yashodhara slept in his arms, each of those nights, with Indrajeet having a tough time controlling his libido. But he was a warrior at heart, a Kshatriya, who can boast not only of strength and valour, but also for their immense patience while holding a siege.

And that's exactly what Indrajeet was doing, holding a siege to his wife's heart.

Yashodhara woke up on the morning after her wedding, a sense of well-being pervading her mind and body. She stretched her arms above her head, then opened her eyes a slit to see the sunlight pouring from the windows, the curtains having been pushed aside.

She got up with a jerk, remembering the events of the night, her eyes going wide even as colour bloomed in her cheeks. The last thing she recalled was that she had gone to sleep in her husband's arms, just like that. Had she really done that—trusted a man enough to spend the whole night in his arms? Yashodhara was finding it difficult to believe. She turned on her side to check the other half of the bed, and was glad to find it empty.

It had been so long, more than a decade, since Yashodhara had had a peaceful night's sleep. Either nightmares bothered her subconscious, or terrible memories dogged her conscious mind. She had so got used to sleeping lightly that she was amazed at the feeling of well-being which she felt this morning.

The colour in her cheeks darkened when she recalled the moment the scream had left her lips the earlier night. It had been building in her gut, rising fast and almost choking her as she tried to control it when she felt Indrajeet's lips at her neck. He had earned the right, hadn't he—to kiss her and make love to her? After all, she had wed him in the presence of so many witnesses. But that hadn't stopped the fear from surfacing. The dreadful feeling she always had when facing an adult male.

Yashodhara had tried hard to force down the scream which had been building within her, biting her lips hard. But she had lost control when she felt his hand on her breast. It wasn't even as if his touch had been painful. But her body or mind hadn't forgotten the memories of the earlier pain. She had completely lost it as the scream left her lips. To add insult to injury, she had fainted too. It was a wonder Indrajeet hadn't disowned her.

The next thing she had known was that she had been lying on the bed. She felt bad denying her husband his conjugal rights. But it seemed as if Yashodhara had no control over her reactions to being touched intimately. She shut her eyes, shaking her head in denial, even as she valiantly tried to hold back the tears which sprang forth. This is exactly the reason why she hadn't wanted to get married. But both her parents—yes, her dead father too—had cornered her into it. There had been no escape from it.

But was it fair to her new husband, Indrajeet?

Yashodhara recalled his behaviour the earlier night. He had been the personification of patience and care. Not one word of reprimand had left his lips. He had obviously carried her to the bed, wiping her face with a damp cloth and giving her water to drink.

Over and above that, he also held her in his arms so that she could sleep well. How had he even guessed that she had a sleeping problem? Yashodhara didn't remember mentioning it to him, ever.

The wonder was that she had felt no fear at all when she fell into his arms last night. The empathy she received from him must have swept away all her fears. And here she was, feeling completely refreshed after sleeping straight for nine hours.

There was a knock and the door opened just as Yashodhara stepped down from the bed. She turned her face to see her husband walk in, a coffee tray in his hands.

"Good morning, Yash," he said cheerfully, a wide smile on his face as his brown eyes ran over her blushing face. "Did you sleep well?"

Feeling breathless, Yashodhara replied, "Good morning, Jeet. Thanks to you, I slept really well."

"Come on then, let's have coffee."

"Can you please give me a few minutes? I need to brush." Without waiting for his answer, Yashodhara rushed into the bathroom and shut the door behind her, leaning her back against it, her heart beating hard.

Her husband Indrajeet looked too handsome for words. How come she had never noticed it earlier? She had only seen that he was good-looking. But this morning, she felt overwhelmed by his demeanour.

She felt torn by the sudden spark of attraction she was feeling for him.

Taking a few deep breaths, Yashodhara had a quick wash before stepping out of the bathroom to join her husband at the other end of the bedroom where he sat on a chair, looking out through the window.

Seeing her, Indrajeet poured the coffee into two cups, adding milk and sugar before handing one to her.

She sipped on her coffee, looking at him warily, and waiting for him to say something about her strange behaviour the earlier night. But she waited in vain as he spoke to her in detail about his plans for the day. "Are you okay with that? Or would you like to do something else?" he asked, looking at her with a look of enquiry on his face.

Was her husband a saint? Yashodhara stared at him reverently, simply nodding her agreement. She spent the whole day, simply enjoying herself, with no fear gnawing at her insides about the forthcoming night. It was an awesome feeling.

6

The four days of honeymooning at the Iravati Heritage Inn in Khempur were the happiest days of Yashodhara's adult life. She learned a lot about the man she had married. Indrajeet was gentle, kind and patient. Also, he treated her as if she was the most precious being on earth.

They went riding every day and took a number of walks around the lush farmland. They even spent some quiet time, reading together. There was a manmade lake that wasn't far from the inn. It had ducks in it. Yashodhara loved to just sit on the bank and watch the ducks, throwing bits of corn to them from time to time. She laughed when they quacked loudly as if they were expressing their gratitude.

"This property isn't all that big," said Indrajeet, pointing out in both directions with his riding crop as they stopped their horses mid-ride to take a look at the land, "just about a hundred and fifty acres. There are seventy families living here. We recently had their homes renovated. With the solar panels installed, they have uninterrupted electricity nowadays." There was pride in his voice as he took her around the property.

"I like the idea of solar panels. Is it very difficult to have them installed? Do we need any special permissions for that?" Yashodhara was keen to have it set up for the Jadeja farmers as well.

"It's not a big deal. And no, you don't need permissions. In fact, the government encourages people to set up solar power projects. Let's go to your fields and see what needs to be done once we get back home. I can help you or give you the contacts if you want to do it yourself."

She liked his attitude. Indrajeet was ready to help, but careful not to step into her space. Wasn't she lucky?

The meals at the inn were delicious. They were simple and sourced from local ingredients, all fresh. The very air was so clean and invigorating.

"I'll grow fat if I eat like this," laughed Yashodhara, stopping the waiter from serving her one more *roti*, even as she spooned the last of the *dal makhni* into her mouth, savouring its rich taste.

Indrajeet grinned. "I don't really think so, not with the miles of walking we've been doing here." She looked perfect in his eyes and felt even more so when he held her in his arms night after night.

"Are you sure? With my kind of big build, it won't take that many kilos to make me huge." She looked down at her plate when she said this. How the hell had the conversation turned towards her figure? She definitely didn't want to draw her husband's attention to it.

What Yashodhara wasn't aware was that her husband was extremely aware of her curvaceous body. He had trained himself to survive on short naps as his aroused body kept him awake most of the time during the nights.

But he could already see the change in his wife. Yashodhara had grown more confident when she spoke to him, not avoiding his eyes as she used to do earlier. She laughed more and appeared chirpy. Indrajeet had a well of patience. He was also extremely determined to have his own way. He didn't want her to look upon it as her conjugal duty to make love to her husband. He was playing a waiting game, wooing his wife at a leisurely pace. He planned to make her his only when he was sure she wanted it as much as him.

It was their last night at the inn. The two of them were lying on the bed facing each other, chatting lazily.

When there was a lull in the conversation, Yashodhara looked at him, going breathless as she studied his handsome features. What would he think of her if he got to know the truth about her? She mentally shook her head. She couldn't tell him. Her mother had made Yashodhara promise that she wouldn't divulge the truth to a living soul.

Indrajeet watched his wife's luscious lips droop. Holding back his hand that was tempted to trace the shape of her mouth and turn the drooping curve upwards, he dragged his eyes up to look into her hazel green gaze. "Is something wrong, Yash? You look unhappy."

Yashodhara sighed, shaking her head. "It was just a passing thought, nothing important."

How much ever she tried to be cheerful, the niggling worry refused to go away. It was obvious to Indrajeet that she was still disturbed. Indrajeet sensed it was best not to push her into a corner. They had come a long way in these four days. He knew asking too many questions would have Yashodhara retreat into her shell once again. He knew she would tell him in her own time, at her own pace.

Indrajeet gathered his wife into his arms, pressing his lips to her forehead. "Go to sleep, sweetheart. Goodnight."

For the first time since the day they had arrived, sleep eluded Yashodhara. She became conscious of the width of her husband's chest which felt rock hard. How can this virile strength feel so comfortable? She turned around, spooning her back against his body, dragging his arm around her waist, snuggling close to him under the comforter, willing sleep to claim her.

Indrajeet bit back his groan as he felt her lush bottom fit snugly against his rising manhood. It was also tough to restrain his hand from straying below her waist. Her gorgeous breasts were too close for comfort and his hand itched to mould their shape. He took a deep breath to calm himself down only to be overwhelmed by the smell which was so unique to Yashodhara—the smell of incense smoke and the woodsy perfume she favoured. It was pure torture.

Indrajeet invoked the Kshatriya spirit from deep within, bringing forth an iron control to his libido. It was no small task, but the prince from the long line of Thakore Royals, managed this herculean task, just as all his ancestors had done before him—wielding total control over his senses.

The next morning, the royal couple went home to a rousing welcome from the Thakores. Ragini Devi was so glad that her eldest born was married, even more so when she saw how happy he appeared to be. Her daughter-in-law, Princess Yashodhara Jadeja, was not just beautiful, but also well-mannered. She had no royal airs. Ragini had worried a lot about that since it was her mother-in-law, the *Rajmata,* who had selected Indrajeet's bride.

Rajmata Santhini Devi had also selected Ragini for her own son, Gajendar. But over the years, she refused to treat Ragini with the respect that she deserved. The older woman's peeve was that her son Gajendar was a slave to his wife's wishes. What she didn't realise was that Ragini was too gentle to dictate anything to her husband or anyone else for that matter. It was just that Gajendar adored his wife and consulted her before every decision he took. The old lady was troubled as she didn't like to think of her husband Gajendar as a weak man. She considered her son to be spineless.

Santhini Devi looked on, a shrewd look in her eyes as Ragini hugged her daughter-in-law. Uff! What did Gajendar see in his wife? Ragini behaved like a commoner, totally unfit to be wed to royalty.

Of course, that she also belonged to the royal family of Himachal Pradesh didn't matter to the *Rajmata*. Ragini was a simpleton, period. Her life revolved around her husband, her two sons and the kitchen. Santhini Devi had refused to let Ragini handle her daughter Dayanita, doing her best to spoil the girl rotten. The matriarch's plan was to bring up her granddaughter in her own image. It looked like she had succeeded too.

Santhini Devi turned to look at her granddaughter Dayanita with fierce pride in her eyes. The girl stood on the side, her body taut with irritation, a pout on her lips and a disdainful expression in her eyes. Perfect! Dayanita was a Thakore through and through. But she was here only on a brief holiday, to attend her brother's wedding. She was leaving the very next day to go back to the University of Georgia, where she was doing her Masters in Communication.

While the *Rajmata* would never admit to it, she missed her granddaughter, especially the times the two of them joined forces to pick on the gentle Ragini. The *Rajmata's* favourite way to pass time was to turn Dayanita against her mother. But then, all of that had reduced to nothing since Indrajeet had returned from Harvard.

The *Rajmata's* irritation towards her eldest grandson had turned to complete admiration over the last four years. He had not only secured her an expensive membership at the club that the royals catered to, but had also restored the Thakore palaces and lands to the state they used to be in the earlier days. More than all that, he resembled his grandfather Devendar Thakore, Santhini Devi's late husband, with each passing day.

There was only one thing that she continued to dislike about Indrajeet nowadays. He worshipped his mother, the docile Ragini. Santhini Devi just couldn't tolerate that. But one could not have everything, she supposed. With a soft sigh, she placed a hand on the newly-weds' heads in turn when they touched her feet to take her blessings.

Gajendar hugged his son close, his throat choked up with joy. While he adored all his offspring, he felt so proud of Indrajeet, blessings overflowing from his heart for his oldest son. Indrajeet had achieved something he himself hadn't been able to. Not only had the palaces been restored to their former beauty, he had also dealt successfully with all the farmers who tilled their lands, using some new techniques to make the stubborn lands yield. Before Indrajeet had taken over, droughts and floods year after year, had taken a toll of the crops. But his son had managed to work wonders, resulting in plenty of healthy crops for everyone.

Gajendar was painfully aware about the fact that his mother had no respect for him or his wife. But he didn't really care. The old lady was a tyrant. Luckily, Indrajeet had trained her to eat out of his hand. Gajendar couldn't help but be amused by that. Nowadays, the *Rajmata* left Gajendar and Ragini in peace, spending more and more time at her club and thank God for that.

He turned to look at his daughter-in-law, a bit surprised that she was still shy. He had heard a lot about Princess Yashodhara. But nothing had prepared him for her timid behaviour. She touched his feet respectfully, but talked only when spoken to. Gajendar turned again to look at his son and was glad to see the joy on his face. As long as Indrajeet was happy, he was comfortable with his daughter-in-law's personality.

Dayanita looked at the scene in front of her eyes, with an expression of absolute boredom on her face. At just a little more than twenty-three, Dayanita was totally cynical, all thanks to her grandmother. What was all the hullabaloo about? Indrajeet had married Yashodhara five days ago. What was there to celebrate today? Didn't everyone have work to do?

Lucky Rajvardhan! He had left to go back to Harvard the very next day after the wedding, insisting that he had to get back to his job, even if he could stay away from college. Dayanita had let her grandmother persuade her to stay a wee bit longer.

Well, it wasn't difficult staying at their palace home these days. It looked so awesome, the marble floor and staircase all polished up, the fresco on the ceilings as good as new, the stained glass windows restored to their original sparkling beauty, new velvet curtains hanging everywhere, the sofas sparkling with brocade covers and silk-covered cushions, so many artefacts, restored and placed strategically all around. These had all been lying in the attic for decades, looking sorry. They brought such beauty to their home, making it the palace it was meant to be.

Dayanita was especially happy since she had so envied the way Ritvik Bansal had renovated the summer palace they had sold him, and converted it into a luxurious five-star hotel. It was all thanks to Indrajeet that they lived in the lap of luxury these days. Well, Rajvardhan had helped too. However, his efforts were minimal compared to what Indrajeet had done.

She now looked at her new sister-in-law. They hadn't had much of a chance to spend time together. Not that Dayanita cared. There was less than a couple of years of difference between the two. Tall herself at five feet, nine inches, Dayanita didn't care for the fact that Yashodhara was taller than her by an inch.

She wrinkled her nose. Did Indrajeet's wife appear a bit masculine? She was not just tall, but had a large figure to match. Checking out her figure once again, Dayanita changed her mind. Not masculine, definitely not. Yashodhara's figure was too well-shaped, totally feminine, to be confused. But wasn't she huge! Dayanita grimaced. Why did she care?! It was Indrajeet's life.

And so, with varying opinions flooding around them from their immediate family, Indrajeet and Yashodhara began their lives together in the Thakore palace.

Jaswantlal Diwekar stared at the ceiling of the prison cell that he was sharing with five other inmates. Another six months to go, the fifty-nine-year-old pacified himself. What did six months matter against the fourteen years—the full length of his prison sentence—which he had been forced to endure?

Just imagine being incarcerated at forty-five! The best period of his life had been spent behind the high walls of this extra secure prison, and it was all thanks to Rani Hyma Devi.

One day, he had been the husband of the Rani of Bhatewar, the ruler of all he surveyed. And that had been no small area. The so-called small kingdom of the Jadejas stretched over five hundred square kilometres. Jaswantlal had had it all—a beautiful wife, a huge palace to live in, sumptuous meals, servants to wait on him hand and foot and more. He didn't have to lift a finger if he didn't choose to.

Then, suddenly out of the blue, his ex-wife Hyma Devi had had him arrested. Bhupinder Sharma, the commissioner of police those days, had acted on Hyma Devi's instructions for sure. Between the two of them, Bhupinder and Hyma Devi had made a watertight case against him for theft and forgery and got him a sentence of life imprisonment. He had lost it all, overnight.

The first few years in the prison, Jaswantlal had harboured a lot of resentment towards his ex-wife. So much so, that he had thought up a number of ways to torture her and her only daughter. But he had had a lot of time to think since then. The prisoners did some hard, physical labour and there was nothing to occupy their minds, unless they chose to read. Jaswantlal wasn't too keen on books. They tended to bore him to tears.

After spending ten years in a state of anger, fate intercepted quietly and uneventfully. A *sadhu* started coming to speak to the prisoners over a week, for a couple of hours in the evening. It was only a handful of the prisoners who showed interest. With nothing much to occupy his mind, Jaswantlal went for the first lecture and was instantly hooked.

He didn't really understand all of what the *sadhu* said. The ascetic spoke a lot about karma, reincarnation, soul searching and the like. What kept Jaswantlal hooked was the *sadhu's* soothing voice, more than the actual words. The peace that had been eluding him for the last ten years, suddenly pervaded his life. He began to sleep better and he felt his anger melting slowly but steadily. The power of the *sadhu's* voice was hypnotic.

The last three days, the *sadhu* touched on the topic of forgiveness and letting go. Jaswantlal began to listen in earnest as it touched his heart which all along was craving revenge. On the second last day, tears poured down his shrunken cheeks as the *sadhu* explained how it was very important to forgive. It was even more important to request forgiveness for one's earlier sins.

It appeared as if redemption wouldn't be all that difficult. Yes, Jaswantlal had committed a terrible act and he needed to ask for forgiveness. And that was the pain which had been festering deep within him. Instead of understanding his stress, he had resorted to anger. He had spent the whole time in jail planning vengeance on Hyma Devi.

Now it was time to repent and ask for forgiveness. If he was sincere, Jaswantlal was convinced that he would receive it too.

Over the next few years, twice he applied for reducing his sentence on the basis of good behaviour. He deserved it as he was probably the only prisoner who didn't resort to violence in this particular jail. But no, his application had been rejected, both times. He was sure it was due to that moron Bhupinder Sharma's interference. The man was the Inspector General of Police nowadays and was constantly keeping a close watch on Jaswantlal.

Jaswantlal turned around on his bed to face the wall with a huge sigh shuddering through him. He would wait, wait for another six months, when his sentence would end. Then he would go to seek forgiveness, in person.

At the time Jaswantlal was repenting his mistake, the Inspector General of Police, Bhupinder Sharma, was having lunch with Rani Hyma Devi at her palace home.

They went back a long way. To begin with, the Rani of Bhatewar had helped him get a promotion in the police force. In return, Bhupinder had helped her by arresting her second husband and ensuring a life sentence for him.

Bhupinder Sharma had been married for seven years before his wife died after a prolonged fight with cancer. Busy with his career, he had never considered getting married again. After the arrest of Rani Hyma Devi's second husband and their subsequent divorce, the two of them—Bhupinder and Hyma Devi—had become close friends, meeting once every few months, for lunch or dinner. Bhupinder found the Rani both intelligent and shrewd, and he took her advice in many matters of the state.

He looked at her now, as he polished off the *gulab jamuns* and *vanilla ice-cream* which they were having for dessert. "Before I forget, Jaswantlal Diwekar would be released in approximately six months."

Her hazel eyes went wide and a gamut of emotions flashed through them as Hyma Devi stared at him. "Is it time for that already?" She whispered softly; shutting her eyes for a few seconds and desperately trying to bring her emotions under control. "Is there no way he can be retained behind bars for longer?"

Bhupinder laughed. "How I wish! But no, Hyma Devi, it won't be possible. The man had applied for parole, not once, but twice. I had to use all my influence to make sure that it wasn't granted. He's finishing his sentence soon. There isn't much we can do now."

Hyma Devi grimaced. "Somehow, I get a bad feeling about this. Jaswant won't keep quiet. He's bound to create trouble." She sighed, thinking that it was but a few weeks since Yashodhara had settled down to a married life. Why the hell did the man have to be released now? "I just hope for all our sakes that I don't end up murdering Jaswant," she declared, her eyes going cold.

Bhupinder patted her hand that was on the table. "Don't worry. It won't come to that, I'm sure." His eyes were gentle as he reassured her.

Even Bhupinder didn't know the reason why Hyma Devi had wanted Jaswantlal placed behind bars fourteen years ago. Her help to get him promoted in the police ranks was not the only reason why Bhupinder had rushed to her aid. It was also because he always sensed the Rani had a strong sense of justice and she would never, ever, misuse her power. The accusations that they had placed on her second husband may not have been true, but Bhupinder had been confident that the man needed to be behind bars. Otherwise, Hyma Devi wouldn't have requested it to be done. In all his years in the police profession, Bhupinder had never met a more honest person than Rani Hyma Devi.

"I sincerely hope not," she laughed, "I definitely don't want to go to jail for murdering that scum, even if he deserves it."

Bhupinder shrugged. "Well, I thought I'd let you know, just in case. Let's just hope he slinks away like the rat he is."

Hyma Devi shook her head. "Not a rat, not Jaswant. More like a fox. He's a wily bastard. But thanks for telling me, Bhupinder. It's good to be forewarned."

Hyma Devi did a lot of thinking once the Inspector General left. She planned to increase the security at the palace. Her instinct was to warn Yashodhara. Then on second thoughts she didn't want her daughter to panic. She had seemed so much at peace when she had been home the other day, along with her husband. No, it wasn't fair to shatter Yashodhara's newfound peace.

She probably might have to take Indrajeet into confidence. Yes, that's what she would do, decided Rani Hyma Devi. No, she didn't plan to tell him the reason; just that Jaswantlal was trouble with a capital T.

8

xcept for the twenty rooms which had been kept aside for the family, the rest of the three-hundred-plus rooms in the Thakore palace were thrown open to the public for all seven days of the week. The entrance to the family home was from the eastern side. A separate set of gates had been built into the wall from that side, for the family to come and go.

The main gate for visitors, which was also the original gate to the palace, faced the north. These rose up to twenty feet in the air and were made of wrought iron. The Thakores' emblem of an elephant in royal refinery, with a *howdah* mounted on its back, was replicated in bronze and affixed, one on each gate. The tour came at a cost, of course, along with an intense security check at the entrance. There were also a number of CCTV cameras placed at strategic points keeping track of the visitors.

Audiotapes were available in multiple languages. Besides Hindi and English, these included a choice of South Indian languages and some European languages as well.

Indrajeet and Yashodhara joined the group of people at the entrance at 10.30 on a Tuesday morning. He had suggested the day tour when he found out that his wife had never seen the palace before.

Tuesdays and Fridays were special at the palace, with a live performance in the hall that used to be the throne room in yonder days.

It had been Gajendar's idea. He had always loved playacting and had roped in his wife Ragini Devi to perform as well. The two of them held court from 11 AM till 1 PM and again from 3 PM to 5 PM on those days.

"If India weren't a republic, Papa would have been the king. You will see both my parents in full regalia today, the whole of the throne room decorated richly like it used to be when my great grandfather was the king."

"What about your grandfather?" Yashodhara asked, looking around her as they walked into a long corridor that seemed to run all around the structure.

"The rule of kings had been abolished at the tail end of my great grandfather's time. My grandfather, Devendar Thakore, became the head of the Thakore royal house in 1954. Of course, during those days, they still had a lot of influence over the government and lived the lives of royalty. You have seen Grandma; she still thinks she lives during the British Raj." Indrajeet grinned before continuing, "The joke is that she was born only in November 1948, all of fifteen months after India gained independence."

Yashodhara smiled back, able to see what he meant. Santhini Devi did flaunt a lot of queenly airs. What Yashodhara didn't mention was that her mother was also a lot similar to the *Rajmata*, even though she was way younger.

They walked through the magnificent rooms, Indrajeet proudly showing her his heritage. The theme of the elephant was predominant in most artefacts. There was an ivory room which was full of ancient artefacts. The ivory had a yellow patina and Indrajeet lovingly explained the age of each piece depending on the sheen on the object. There was a bronze room, another room full of weapons used by the Thakores over the past four centuries—swords, curved knives, bows and arrows, spears, javelins and more. There was a silver room and one that consisted of different types of *howdahs*—carriers that went on the back of an elephant—made of sandalwood combined with ivory, silver, bronze and there was even a golden *howdah* which was kept in a glass case with an electronic lock. There were velvet cushions and tassels to add flamboyance to the pieces.

"Most of the wares on display had been left under cloth covers and ignored over at least two decades. Maintaining them, as you must be aware, is no easy feat. It took an army of workmen almost a year to restore them to their original state, or at least as close to that as possible." Indrajeet looked around at his heritage, his heart overflowing with gratitude that he could manage to make it what it was today.

While the Thakores' property in land, buildings, heirlooms and jewellery ran to about twenty thousand crore rupees, their cash had dwindled to the last few lakhs a decade ago. It had been his father's idea to sell the summer palace—for which the *Rajmata* was yet to forgive him—and get things back on its feet.

A bell rang in the background, before an announcement was made through hidden speakers, that the court was to begin in a few minutes. "Come along. Let's not miss the Maharaja and Maharani walk into the throne room." Indrajeet took his wife's hand and walked swiftly towards the centre of the palace.

They entered the throne room from a side door. Taking a couple of steps inside, Yashodhara gasped. From a royal family herself and having lived in a palace more than half her life, she still wasn't prepared for the grandeur of the Thakore palace throne room. It was truly a feast for the eyes.

The marble-floored, rectangular hall with a long red carpet running down the middle from the wide-open front door till the marble steps—there were fifteen of those—that led up to the twin thrones, was about eight thousand square feet with a twenty-five foot high frescoed ceiling.

Looking up, Yashodhara was startled, her eyes going wide open as she took in the number of chandeliers that hung from the high ceiling, glowing with LED lights, throwing light on the fresco which was typically local with Mughal influences. She turned when she heard the beat of the drums and the blare of trumpets as a procession of men and women wearing colourful clothes walking on both sides of the red carpet. The women carried trays of rose petals that they scattered over the carpet for the royal couple to walk on. A man wielding a microphone called the visitors' attention to the Maharaja and Maharani who walked sedately down the length of the carpet.

Gajendar wore a knee length *sherwani* of cream and gold over a pristine white dhoti, his feet encased in gold embroidered *mojiris*. A bejewelled turban of pink and gold sat on his head while a cummerbund held his long sword in an intricately carved silver scabbard.

"Ragini Aunty looks stunning. I wouldn't have recognised her as the lady who supervises the battalion of servants at our home, wearing a simple printed silk sari with minimal jewellery." Yashodhara spoke to Indrajeet in a whisper, awe in her voice as she stared at her mother-in-law.

Ragini Devi's bearing was regal as she walked down the red carpet, wearing a hand-woven *Jaipuri Bandhej* silk sari in deep pink which was heavily embroidered in pure gold *zari*. She wore her hair in a low chignon with a golden half-crown set with diamonds sitting prettily on her head.

She wore multiple gold chains and necklaces sporting precious gems that shimmered under the light from the chandeliers. More people walked behind the royal couple, with a distance of five feet separating them.

The retinue reached the marble stairs at the other end of the hall. The musicians and flower ladies separated to walk to the two sides of the hall while the king and queen walked up the steps, Gajendar taking his wife's hand and tucking it into the crook of his elbow.

They reached the elaborate throne made of sandalwood and decorated with ivory, gold and precious stones. Intricately carved elephants faced the front and served as armrests on the throne. The royal couple could rest their arms on the top of the *howdahs* on the elephants' backs.

Indrajeet looked on; a smile in his face, aware of how much his father enjoyed the show. His mother had been reluctant in the beginning, but had started liking the *durbar* that was held regularly on Tuesdays and Fridays for the benefit of visitors.

Raja Gajendar Thakore raised his right hand to the crowd who acknowledged his presence with an applause. Many farmers and merchants who lived locally made it a point to visit their king during the *durbar* sessions, enjoying the old world feel to the atmosphere. There were a number of foreigners in the audience too.

A small stage was set up not far from the dais where the royals were seated. Musicians and singers settled down there before elaborately costumed dancers walked into the throne room and took their positions in the middle of the hall. Soon, they were gyrating to the beats of drums and trumpets while folk singers joined the melee, singing popular Rajasthani songs.

The crowds sitting on both sides of the hall and at the back roared appreciatively as the song and dance sequence came to an end about half an hour later.

Simulated cases were brought before the king with two parties arguing their respective sides until the king gave his judgement, after consulting his queen and the half a dozen ministers who sat on both sides of the hall, not far from the royal couple. It was truly entertaining and Yashodhara was startled to see that it was already 1 PM and the *durbar* was being dismissed.

The royal couple stepped down the stairs and walked the length of the hall to leave the throne room through the front door.

"That was simply awesome, Jeet. I'm so glad that we got to see it. The scene sure took me down the pages of history." There was admiration on Yashodhara's face as she turned to talk to her husband with glowing eyes.

"Isn't it? When Papa first suggested the idea, I had a few misgivings. But after just one session, I was floored. I've been to dozens of these shows, but never tire of watching it."

"I'm sure. I'd love to come again too."

"Sure. Shall we proceed to the lunch table? The royal kitchen and dining area have been converted into a restaurant serving authentic Rajasthani cuisine. I'm sure you'll enjoy both the food and the ambience."

Yashodhara tucked her hand into her husband's arm as they walked across the throne room and stepped out into another room, in the same direction in which the visitors were going. All were obviously headed for lunch.

She literally gaped when they entered the royal dining room. Long and narrow carpets were spread in lengths across the long room, with carved, square, low wooden tables placed in the front, one table per diner. Some people were already sitting on the floor on the carpets and waiting for food to be served.

"The half with the green carpets is for vegetarian meals. The other side with the red carpets is for non-vegetarians. There's another dining room to that side." Indrajeet pointed to a door across. "There are proper dining tables there, for those who don't want to sit on the floor."

"This is so lovely. Shall we have vegetarian today? If you don't mind, that is." She looked at her husband in enquiry.

Indrajeet shrugged, "Why not?"

He guided her to one side and they settled down on the green carpet. A waiter walked by with a large copper kettle and another with a bowl. The visitors could wash their hands before beginning their meals.

The two of them washed their hands in the warm water, Yashodhara thanking the waiters sweetly before wiping her hands on the cloth napkin that was placed along with a tall brass tumbler of cool water.

Another waiter carried shiny brass plates with half a dozen bowls on each one and placed them on the low tables, one each in front of every guest. A line up of four waiters served the food consisting of sliced cucumber, tomato, carrots and onions, two types of pickles, three types of chutneys, *aloo gobhi*, *gatte ki sabzi*, *aloo pyaaz*, *papad churi*, *aam ki kadhi*, *kanji vada*, *pancharatna dal*, *mini samosa* and *palak bhajia*. Along with these, they were served *methi bajra pooris*, *masala tikadia* and *Kathiawadi kichadi*. There was *mohanthal* and *malpuas* to satisfy the sweet cravings, all washed down with glasses of *chaas* which was available in plenty.

While Indrajeet did full justice to the meal, Yashodhara nibbled at everything. "Oh no, this is a lot of food," she protested when Indrajeet asked her if she would have one more *poori*.

"I know. It's exactly what royalty used to consume in those days. But then again, people tended to get more physical exercise then which probably justified eating such a variety," he grinned, drinking from his glass of *chaas*.

"Of course, I feel like a long walk to help me digest all this," she retorted with a slight smile on her face.

He got up to give her a hand to help her get up. "Are you up to seeing more of the palace or have you had enough for today?"

"I'd like to see more, if you aren't bored."

"Never that!

The two of them continued to tour the palace and only left at closing time. Yashodhara was absolutely enamoured by the palace and Indrajeet was so glad his wife had enjoyed the tour.

Still they had managed to see only one third of the palace, deciding to come again the next week.

The two of them fell into a comfortable routine. They went riding almost every day, sometimes just to watch the sunrise, many times to oversee the farmlands. Yashodhara had spoken to him about the difficulties that her mother faced while dealing with the young farmers who refused to listen to her suggestions. Installation of solar panels had already begun on the Jadeja farm, another thing that Yashodhara felt grateful to her husband for.

She had been truly impressed with the hostel he had created out of the adjoining buildings of the palace. People who came to Udaipur to study or work had a difficult time getting a place to stay. It was either too expensive or they had no facility for regular meals. Indrajeet had come up with a winning combination of both at a sustainable rate and the facility with some forty rooms and half a dozen dormitories which could accommodate ten people each, was filled to capacity most of the time.

It was roughly a month later when Yashodhara knocked on the library door at about eleven in the morning. She was aware Indrajeet was working at his desk that day.

She stepped into the library, her heart beating hard as she turned breathless. She had a similar reaction, every time she came face-to-face with her husband. She had kind of accepted that and even begun to look forward to the exhilaration which overcame her every time she set her eyes on him.

"Hey, come on in. What's up?" Indrajeet greeted her.

She walked up to his desk and perched on one corner, not far from him. "Just. I'm done with my work and wanted to check if you needed something done." Yashodhara looked into his warm brown gaze as she spoke to him, feeling colour steal into her cheeks as she noticed the banked heat there. An inadvertent sigh shuddered through her body, startling her in its unexpectedness.

"What was that for?" Indrajeet's dark eyebrow went up in query as it touched his hairline.

Yashodhara clenched her hands into fists to restrain her fingers from running through his hair. He had no qualms about brushing her hair almost every night, just before they went to sleep. But she had never dared to touch him. She was shaken by the strong feeling of temptation, so compelling that she clenched her fists all the harder.

Seeing her discomfort, Indrajeet took her fist which was closest to him in both his hands and looked deeply into her hazel green eyes. Opening her fingers one by one, he pressed his lips to the palm of her hand, stroking it lightly with a damp tongue.

Yashodhara was surprised to realise that the moaning sound had come from her throat when Indrajeet lifted his head to look up at her. "You said something?" he asked, mischief and desire warring in his eyes.

She shook her head, feeling weak with longing. For what? For him to kiss her palm once again? The touch of his tongue had been explosive, making her heart go crazy as it was beating at such a rapid pace.

"Yash... talk to me." He took her other hand also, opening the fist and kissing her right palm.

Yashodhara shivered, goose bumps breaking out all over her flesh. She shut her eyes, savouring the sensation of his tongue stroking the centre of her palm, the unfamiliar sensation of her tightening breasts catching her unawares.

She opened her eyes in a hurry, highly disturbed, her gaze falling on the back of her husband's head as he bent over her hands. Completely unaware of what she was doing, Yashodhara pulled her left hand out of his loose grip and ran her fingers through the silky tresses of his hair, shutting her eyes again as the tactile sensation hit her hard. Her fingers slid through his hair in a caress as she continued to run her hand over his head, unable to stop herself.

Indrajeet drew his chair closer and pressed his face to her thigh, thrilled at his wife's overture. This was the first time she had voluntarily caressed him and it felt so awesome, her slender fingers running through his hair, fluttering over his scalp. He groaned when he felt her hand at the back of his neck, burrowing his face against her right thigh, his hand pressed flat over the left one.

Yashodhara lifted her hand off him, startled. Was he in pain? Why had he groaned? Had she done something wrong?

"Why did you stop?" Indrajeet lifted his head to ask her.

She felt bereft when the warmth of his face was removed from her thigh, even as she shook her head. "I... did I hurt you?" Her voice was hesitant as she stared into his bloodshot eyes. What had happened to bring that on so suddenly? He had been perfectly alright a few minutes ago.

Indrajeet smiled, gently touching her cheek with his hand. "Of course not. Is that why you stopped? Because you thought you hurt me?" When she nodded, he continued, "It takes more than your gentle touch on my head to injure me." Grinning, he took her hand and placed it on his shoulder. "May I have a kiss?"

Yashodhara looked deeply into her husband's chocolate eyes, totally mesmerised. Placing the other hand also on his left shoulder, she pressed her mouth to his manly cheek, her lashes fluttering against her cheeks as every nerve-end on her lips came alive the moment they touched him. Copying his gesture earlier, she opened her mouth to press the tip of her tongue to his cheek, stroking it back and forth. The next second, she found herself falling into his lap, her arms circling his neck to hold on for dear life.

"Jeet..." Yashodhara buried her face against his neck, colour flaming over her cheeks. What had come over her? Her tongue tingled from the memory of brushing against his rough cheek. Her body felt hot and then cold as she shivered in his arms. She didn't quite understand what she wanted.

His hand in her hair, Indrajeet pulled her face up to his and pressed his lips to her quivering mouth. He gently sucked on her lower lip, his tongue stroking it rhythmically back and forth. He shifted his attention to her upper lip and caressed it before pressing his tongue into her mouth, his body shuddering with the sensations swamping him. "You taste so good," he growled against her lips, his tongue tracing the contours of her mouth before lazily rubbing against hers. "Yash..."

Yashodhara felt herself drowning in unfamiliar sensations. She felt breathless and buoyant at the same time, thinking that she might just float away in a tide of sensuality. Is this what love-making was all about? She moaned in protest when Indrajeet removed his mouth from hers to bury his face against her neck. She didn't want him to stop kissing her. But what was he doing? His lips were at her neck, his tongue stroking over her pulse there. She shivered at the sensations he invoked in her body, her hands clutching his wide shoulders.

"Touch me, Yash," Indrajeet invited her, opening the top buttons of his shirt.

Yash braced her hands on his shoulders, before opening slumberous green eyes to gaze at him. Her gaze dropped down to his wide chest to stare in curious wonder at the abundance of whorls of dark hair liberally spread on his chest. She could see his strong throat working as he waited patiently for her to respond. Unable to resist any more, Yashodhara took her right hand off his shoulder and pressed her open hand flat against his chest, a tremor passing through her at the impact of touching all that bare skin. Eager to explore, she rubbed her hand over his naked chest, pushing the lapels of his shirt out of her way. She brought down her left hand to join her right as she unfastened the rest of the buttons on his shirt, running her hands from his shoulders down to his abdomen, unaware of the mewling noises she made in her throat.

Indrajeet let her have her way with him before holding both her hands together in one of his. "I think it's my turn. What say?" His voice was a growl as his body was roused to a fever pitch by her soft strokes.

"Huh?!" Yashodhara stared up at his face as if she had just remembered him, her eyes glazed over. "What?"

He gave her a weak grin. "Do you like touching me?"

"Hmm, mmm." Colour stole over her cheeks as she met his eyes in a shy gaze.

"Wouldn't you say it's only fair for me to touch you as well?"

She stared at him as if trying to grasp what he was saying before the colour drained from her face, leaving her pale and breathless. "Jeet... I... will you please let go of me?" She tried to get off his lap.

"No. I don't want to let you go." His voice was firm as he continued to hold her hazel green gaze, refusing to let her off his lap.

"Please Jeet!" She was pleading now, a thin film of tears forming in her eyes, breaking his heart.

Indrajeet took his arms from around her waist, saying, "Have it your way."

Though he didn't say anything else, she could feel the tension in his body. He must definitely be angry with her by now. She could feel it in the way his thighs had tightened under her. But what could she do? She watched sadly as he buttoned his shirt, hiding his magnificent chest from her view. And she didn't like it. She wanted to push his hands away and pull open the buttons and remove his shirt. She wanted the freedom to touch her husband and feel his muscles rippling under her hands. Desire and fear warred within her. The moment she had refused to let him touch her intimately, she had lost the right to touch him in a similar manner.

With great temerity, Yashodhara continued to sit on his lap. Her nervousness was obvious in her twisting hands. But then, she had been landed with a major problem by now. She very well knew there was more to the physical side of marriage than a few kisses. But... but she wasn't physically or mentally equipped to make her husband happy. Then again, she couldn't deny her enjoyment every time she kissed him. Touching his bare chest today had been explosive. Would he understand if she spoke to him about it?

"Jeet?" Her voice was a whisper as she tried to catch her husband's eye.

He gave her a look bordering on cold, the earlier warmth having completely disappeared from his brown eyes. Not that she could blame him. "Is it something urgent? Or can it wait until lunch time? I have some urgent work to finish."

Her face darkened with rejection. Giving him a small nod, Yashodhara slipped off his lap to stand on trembling legs. Would her treacherous legs manage to get her across the room and outside the door? She wasn't too sure.

Indrajeet looked surreptitiously at the woman standing next to him, feeling the tremors shaking her only too well. He shut his eyes in frustration. She had responded so well to his kisses. And her hands fluttering over his chest before she gained enough confidence to stroke him had driven him crazy with longing. He hadn't wanted a repeat of the screaming fit on their wedding night and that's the reason he had asked her permission to touch her. Night after night, holding her sensuous and voluptuous body wasn't exactly easy on him.

Was his wife just using him? Indrajeet shook his head and realised he was being way too suspicious. She was too innocent for that. There was something there. Was she maybe feeling too shy to tell him what her problem was?

"Yash…" He took her hand in his just when she stepped away from him, stopping her in her tracks.

"Jeet." She turned her head to look at him over her shoulder.

"Do you want to talk about it?"

"About what?" Her voice trembled with the tears she was holding back.

He got up to gather her in his arms, unable to see her so unhappy. "I love you, Yash. I want us to be happy together. But I also want to make love to you, worship you with my body. I want to touch you, intimately." His lips were close to her ear as he whispered the words. "You enjoyed us kissing, didn't you?"

She nodded, turning around to bury her face in his chest. "I did, I do. I like touching you too."

Indrajeet smiled on hearing that. "I promise you that you will like being touched too. Shall we give it a try?"

She looked up at him, fear in her eyes. "Are you sure you won't hurt me?"

"Why sweetheart? Why do you think I'll hurt you? In all the time you've known me, have I done anything to cause you pain?"

She allowed herself to make contact with the warmth emanating from his eyes. He had always cared for her. He had been a selfless giver. She swallowed briefly and felt a choking sensation in her throat. Should she let him touch her breasts? It was just that her mind refused to let go of the accumulated grief and anguish. What should she do? Yashodhara opened her eyes to look at her husband. She had truly tried his patience in the five weeks of their marriage. And he hadn't complained even once. She took his hand and pressed her lips to his palm before bringing it close to her body and placing it against her breast, her breath coming out in gasps as she shut her eyes tightly, waiting for the pain to follow.

Indrajeet's touch was gentle as he curled his right hand over her left breast, his palm against the tip. He stroked gently, delighted to feel the nipple swell and harden in response, careful not to apply pressure. He didn't want his wife running away, scared. "Kiss me, Yash."

She raised her face up to his, her eyes glazed over at the unfamiliar sensations taking over her body as she felt him squeeze her breast gently. So much so, she took his left hand and placed it over her right breast, thrilled to see the smile on his face. "I like your touch," she whispered against his lips before pressing her mouth to his. Hesitantly, she drew her tongue against his lips only to gain entry into his mouth immediately. It was like plunging headlong into a soft, warm pool on a cold, winter night. She revelled in the sensations as she delved into his mouth while he continued to explore the shape of her breasts over her sari, blouse and bra. And it was pure bliss!

What would it feel like if he touched her skin in that case? Yashodhara couldn't wait to find out, recalling how much she had enjoyed touching his bare chest. Feeling too shy to tell him, she moved away to look up at her husband, burgeoning desire in her hesitant gaze.

A dark eyebrow went up to touch his hairline as Indrajeet gazed at her with a smile, a look of enquiry on his face.

It was all too new for her. Too shy to tell him in words, Yashodhara pulled at the buttons of his shirt, opening them eagerly, driven by the need to touch him.

"Does that mean what I think you mean?" There was gentle laughter in his voice as he looked at her intense face.

Her gaze met his in a flash as she nodded her head before burying her face in his bare chest.

Laughing, Indrajeet lifted her up in his arms to carry her over to the couch on the other side of the library, sitting her down gently before discarding his shirt completely, egged on by her greedy gaze as she studied his body, forgetting to feel shy.

He sat on the couch and lifted her on to his lap. Yashodhara helped him by removing the pearl brooch holding her chiffon sari at her shoulder, turning her head to catch his gaze shyly. He pulled the knot of the string holding her blouse together at the back of her neck, his hands trembling in their eagerness as he pressed his lips to her bare back, stroking his tongue over the top of her spine.

"Jeet…" Her voice was a whisper as she leaned into his chest, revelling in the rasp of his damp tongue down her bare back.

He brought his hands forward to cup her breasts before pulling the blouse off her chest, having removed the two hooks holding it in place at her lower back. The inbuilt bra came away with the blouse and his hands made contact with bare flesh.

Yashodhara's mind worked furiously as she waited for the panic to hit her, her eyes tightly closed as she felt his hands on her breasts. What she felt was something entirely different. Her breasts swelled up to fill his large hands and revelled in his touch as he brushed his thumbs gently over the burgeoning tips, his face buried in her neck. He squeezed gently and stroked softly, making her simply melt into a puddle in his arms.

Had she died and gone to heaven? How could a man's intimate touch on her upper body feel this good? Yashodhara pressed her back against his bare chest as she sat on his lap, her hands clinging to his forearms, her head thrown back against his shoulder. "Jeet…" she moaned. "I love it. Thank you." She turned her head to press her lips to his hard cheek. "I never thought it could be like this."

"Well," he laughed softly, turning his face to press his lips to hers, his hands continuing to caress her twin globes, "this is but the tip of the iceberg."

Yashodhara bent down to see his golden-brown hands caressing her pale flesh, finding the sight too erotic for words. She was zapped by the unfamiliar sensation of wetness between her legs when Indrajeet kneaded her swollen nipples between his thumbs and forefingers. The more he caressed her, the more she craved. For what? She was just drowning in the exquisite sensations as she thrashed her legs on the couch.

He turned her back over his arm before bending down to take the tip of her right breast in his mouth, dragging a damp tongue gently over it, making his wife jump in his arms. He lifted his head to look down at her. "What?" he asked, "Don't you like it?"

"Please. Don't. Stop," she moaned, her eyes open in a half slit.

Grinning, he bent down and continued to make love to her luscious breasts with his wicked hands and lips and tongue. He kept his teeth out of the equation. That would be for later, he promised himself. One step at a time!

Indrajeet was yet to find out what had made Yashodhara shy away from lovemaking. That his wife was a passionate woman was very obvious. But somehow, he didn't think she was ready to go all the way.

He blew softly over the wet tip of her breast, watching it pucker in response, grinning when he heard her moan again. He had come a long way today in breaking her inhibitions.

That night, when they slept in each other's arms, they did away with their pajama tops. Yashodhara was still undecided about what was more exciting—the feel of her husband's mouth on her breasts or the sensation of having them crushed against his hairy chest. She turned around a few times, making Indrajeet groan with need, totally unaware of what she was doing to him. She grinned at him before pulling his head down to her chest, deciding that she preferred his mouth on her as he suckled her deeply.

Hearing a sound of protest, Indrajeet opened his eyes with a jerk, to see his wife struggling in his arms which were holding her close, his face buried against her breasts. She was making a keening noise in her throat as she tried hard to escape his strong hold. A startled look on his face, Indrajeet immediately removed his arms from around her, shaking his head in a daze. "Did I hurt you?" he asked in a horrified voice when he saw the terror in her eyes.

Yashodhara looked at her husband, the panic receding slowly from her face as she shook her head. He had obviously been dreaming and she didn't want to know what it had been about. He had held her tightly in his arms, his face buried in her breasts while his mouth had been seeking her nipples. She had come awake suddenly from a deep sleep and had been completely horrified. In all the nights since they were married, Indrajeet had held her in his protective arms that had only soothed her, unlike today.

"You were dreaming, I think."

Shucks! Indrajeet wanted to break something in frustration. Yes, he realised now that he had been dreaming. But it had felt so real, capturing the tip of her breast in his mouth and suckling it. His aroused body protested as he got up from the bed and walked towards the bathroom, not saying a word to his wife.

She had caught the pain on his face and felt her heart splinter. She was falling for her husband, slowly but surely. It was not just his looks, but the way he treated her, with so much love and care. But she could never give him physical love. Was it fair to him? Maybe she should let him go and encourage him to find another wife. Wouldn't that be the right thing to do?

Yashodhara lifted a pillow and threw it hard, as far away from her as possible, giving vent to her frustration, her anger turning towards her mother. Hadn't she been leading a peaceful life of a single woman?! Why the hell had her mother insisted on getting her married?

So, what if the farmers refused to listen to them? They could have just sold the damn lands and washed their hands off them. That would have definitely been an easier solution. She got up from the bed and walked to the window, looking out at the garden. It was still dark. The radium clock on the marble mantelpiece showed the time to be quarter to four in the morning.

Only she felt wide awake now. It was not just her mind which was awake, but her body too. Her breasts still tingled from the pressure of Indrajeet's face buried against them. While she had been shaken awake by the inherent fear residing within her for years, some instinct prompted her to react with defiance; Yashodhara also realised the warmth and weight of his head against her body had felt too damn good. She was missing it badly now.

Indrajeet stood under the cold shower for more than twenty minutes, willing his manhood to calm down. He raised his face up to the sluice of water falling forcefully from the shower, uncaring that it was the middle of winter. His body felt hot! He also felt wide awake. Suddenly coming to a decision, he turned off the shower and pulling a towel from the rack, dried himself. Finding a fresh pair of shorts and t-shirt on the shelf beneath the wash-basin, he pulled them on and walked out, rubbing the towel over his wet hair.

Yashodhara turned when she heard the bathroom door open and stared at her husband as he stepped out, her throat choking with emotion. He was so handsome and was also adorable. She personally had done nothing in her life to deserve him.

And it was high time she told him so. Her heart breaking with the decision she had arrived at, she walked across the room to stand next to her husband before saying, "We need to talk."

"Exactly what I've been thinking." There was no smile on Indrajeet's face. "Though let me get us some green tea first." His throat felt dry. He walked to a wooden stand near the wardrobe and added water to the electric kettle and switched it on. Picking up two mugs, he placed the green tea-bags in them. Pouring the boiling water into the mugs, he carried them to the table near the window. "Come on, Yash, come and sit down here."

Yashodhara, who had been watching her husband's movements warily, walked over and perched on the tip of the chair across from where he was standing, picking up the mug and warming her hands against the sides. *Wasn't he going to sit?* she thought as he towered over her.

"Yash..."

"Jeet..."

Both started talking together and then stopped at the same time. Indrajeet sat down abruptly and said, "Go on. You have a go first."

Yashodhara sipped from her mug, shutting her eyes for a few seconds to gather her scattered thoughts together. She opened them again, saying, "Jeet, I know that I should have told you this before now. But... I'm sorry. Please accept my sincere apologies. I..."

"What are you talking about?" A deep frown gathered on Indrajeet's forehead as he stared at her.

She took a shuddering breath before continuing, "I should have never married you. No, let me be clear. It's not you. I should never have got married, period. Marriage is not for me. I'm unfit to have a physical relationship with any man. I…"

"And why is that? I don't think you are a lesbian, are you?" Light humour tinged his brown gaze as he eyed her over his tea mug.

"What?" Yashodhara looked amazed as she shook her head vigorously. "Of course, I am not. I…"

"Then why do you say that you are unfit to have a physical relationship with any man? Forget any man. Why can't you have a relationship with me, your husband? I don't think you find me repulsive. Then what's the problem? Do you fear the act itself? Yash, listen to me. We don't need to do it all at one go. We can take it one step at a time. We…" He stopped when he saw her shaking her head vigorously.

"It won't work, Jeet."

"And why won't it work?" There was anger in his voice now as he banged the mug down on the table with a thud.

"Jeet." There were tears in her eyes. "I'm sorry, Jeet. I know it's not fair on you. As I said to you before, I shouldn't have married you. I wish I could just go back in time and change the situation. I…"

"What if I tell you this thought has never crossed my mind? I'm truly happy being married to you. I have absolutely zero regrets."

"How could that even be possible?" Yashodhara jumped up from her chair and began to walk along the length of the window, too restless to sit down. "You must surely hate me. I haven't done anything to make you happy." She stopped in her tracks, tears streaming down her eyes. "I haven't even been a wife to you in the real sense."

Indrajeet got up too, to walk to her and pull her into his arms. Pushing her head into the crook of his shoulder, he stroked her back gently, saying, "Forget about hating you. I love you, Yash. And I don't need you to *do* something to make me happy. I'm happy because you are here with me, as my life partner. Do you understand that?"

With great effort, she wrenched away from him, her heart shattering into a million pieces. "That's not possible, Jeet. You probably think you love me only because we have been with each other for a little more than a month. What about five years later? What when we grow old and you realise you haven't had any children, only because your wife wouldn't let you make love to her? What if you begin to hate me in the future?" She shook her head again. "I think it's best if we get this marriage annulled and you get yourself a proper wife, one who loves you the way you deserve to be loved."

"You mean you don't love me?" Indrajeet challenged softly, a gentle look in his gaze.

The tears flowed faster on hearing that. She turned away from him, her arms crossed tightly over her trembling body. "Please don't complicate matters any further. I can't keep on hurting you."

He took the few steps to hug her from behind. "It's the only thing which matters. Everything else is secondary. So, do you love me or no?"

"Jeet, listen to me. You are too nice a person and you deserve someone who's way better than me. Let me leave you. Believe me, it's for the best."

"And that will make you a happy person for the rest of your life? Will you be at peace living away from me?" Ignoring her pained whimpers, he continued to drive his point home. "And you really think it would be fair to another woman if I get married to her while I'm in love with you? What do you think I am, Yash? Some animal who is driven only by the need for sex?"

Yashodhara turned around with a jerk to stare at him, abject shock in her hazel-green eyes. "Jeet... you know I didn't mean that."

"So! Tell me exactly what you mean. Let me understand." His hands kneaded her shoulders as he refused to let go of her.

She shook her head again. "I don't know what to say." She bent her head down and rested her forehead against his shoulder, not having the strength to argue with him anymore. "I only hope you don't regret your decision. I..." She lifted her head up to look at him. "I don't think you really understand the gravity of the situation, Jeet. I can't make love with you. I'm... I..."

Indrajeet sighed. Finally! Finally, they were going to talk about the reason for her inhibitions. "May I know why? I can feel your heart beating wildly for me. I know for a fact you love me. Then what is stopping you? Even if you don't care to talk to men or look at them in the eye, I know we both have come a long way for you to feel the same way about me." He wouldn't let her escape his sharp gaze as he looked deeply into her eyes.

"I can't tell you why. Just know that I can't make love with you." There was a mutinous look on her face now.

"That's not really fair, Yash. You know it's not just idle curiosity driving me. If I'm to help you at all, I need to know what's troubling you. Tell me!" His voice was commanding. "Did someone touch you inappropriately?"

She turned away, escaping the pull of his mesmerising eyes with great difficulty. "I can't tell you."

"Did someone force himself on you?"

"Shut up, Jeet." Anger shone from the hazel green eyes now. "How many times do I have to tell you some things cannot be put into words? I'm bound by a promise never to speak about anything. Don't. Ask. Me. EVER!"

Indrajeet appeared startled at first before he smiled. Good! It was better to keep her angry instead of tearful. He had obviously hit too close to home. And then, a slow anger surged within him as he gradually grasped the implications of the heart-wrenching situation. Someone had obviously forced himself on Yashodhara. That much was obvious. He would murder the bastard with his bare hands!

"And who the hell would extract such a promise from you?" Indrajeet was also shouting by now. "Is it the same bastard who molested you?"

"No! Don't ask me any more questions. I refuse to answer them." She tried hard to sound brave, but her voice trembled as she said, "Please Jeet."

"Listen to me, Yash. I want us both to have a happy married life, until death us do part. Do you want the same?" There was infinite patience in Indrajeet's voice while the truth was that he wanted to commit murder, maybe a double murder at that—the man who had done that to her and the moron who had made her promise not to talk about it.

She looked at him longingly, before nodding her head, her face pinched. "Yes."

"Have you ever spoken to anyone about what happened to you?"

She shook her head, the pallor in her cheeks increasing.

"Not one single soul?" Indrajeet was astounded.

Yashodhara shook her head, her arms hugging her shivering body, as she recalled the event with crystal clarity.

"Then who took such a ridiculous promise from you? Who tried to enforce this silence?" He wasn't shouting. But he might as well be for the sharpness with which the questions hit Yashodhara.

Could she tell him? Would she not be betraying her mother? "Jeet... I..." Yashodhara tried to prevaricate.

"I'll get to the bottom of it, Yash, whether you choose to tell me or not. I won't leave any stone unturned, till I get to the bottom of the matter. I need my wife—which will ALWAYS remain you—to be happy. I won't rest until I see the fear and stress recede from your eyes," he swore. "Who forced you to make such a promise?" Indrajeet demanded once again.

Yashodhara's expression was pitiable as she looked appealingly at her adamant husband. It slowly dawned on her that he was fighting for her and not against her. She had thought it was best to leave him and let him get on with his life, but apparently, he was determined they stay together and make a happy life with each other. Even if there was a small chance that he would get his way, then her life promised to be the most amazing one. Should she risk giving him an honest reply? But then, she realised she didn't really have a choice.

"It was my mother." Her voice was a hoarse whisper.

T he next day, Indrajeet accompanied his mother-in-law to take a round of the Jadeja farms. That was only a pretext as he was biding his time before talking to Rani Hyma Devi about the promise she had taken from her daughter. Even after admitting that it was her mother who had make her swear not to talk about the incident, Yashodhara had refused to say one more word on the matter. Indrajeet still didn't know what had happened to her. And he was of the strong opinion that she would be healed of her inhibitions only after she got it out of her system.

The wheat and barley farms were not in good shape. The fruit orchards weren't too bad, but not giving the best yield, according to Hyma Devi. When they crossed the farms nearer to the palace and reached the fields on the outskirts, Indrajeet stopped the car and drew down the window to study the crops. These were neither wheat nor barley.

"What all do you grow on your farms, Aunty?" Indrajeet asked as he turned to Hyma Devi.

Hyma Devi looked at him with disapproval, though she didn't say it in words. She had never expected this from the eldest grandson of *Rajmata* Santhini Devi—him calling her 'Aunty'. Her son-in-law had no princely airs. He was too casual. Why hadn't she guessed it when he had visited her palace for the first time? He had been wearing jeans and a linen shirt which had been left open at the throat. That must have told her something. But Hyma Devi had presumed that Indrajeet, being the *Rajmata's* blood, would be royal to the core.

He definitely had a winning personality. She couldn't deny that. Her daughter had fallen madly in love with Indrajeet Thakore was another plus in his favour. Every time she spoke about her husband, there was an excited zing in Yashodhara's voice which had been missing for so many years. And the way he had turned around the account books of the Thakores from red to black, with the figure reaching up to a couple of billions was truly amazing. Oh yes, Hyma Devi had her sleuths. While she didn't have the exact figures, she had a fairly good idea. This was the one reason why she had sent a proposal for the Thakore scion's hand.

Today, Indrajeet had offered to check out their farms, at Yashodhara's behest. And Hyma Devi was accompanying him as her daughter wasn't keen to be among so many farmers, all men. Hyma Devi sighed. She didn't think her daughter was ever going to recover from her trauma and finally become brave enough to face men. She probably should thank her lucky stars Yashodhara was experiencing a normal married life. Hyma Devi had no clue about what was actually happening between the newlywed couple. Nor did she plan to ask. She was always one to bury issues under the carpet and expect them to disappear. The only time she had taken a firm stand was when she had organised the arrest and sentencing of her ex-husband, Jaswantlal Diwekar. Simply because there had been no choice. She couldn't think of any other way to get rid of the man. She was also extremely clear she couldn't keep both her second husband and her young daughter under the same roof, not after what had transpired.

Now, she turned to her son-in-law and said, "It's predominantly wheat and barley, with sugarcane grown in some sections. There are a couple of hundred acres dedicated to fruit orchards where guava, pomegranate, gooseberry and *sapota* trees are grown. There may be some vegetable plots. I'm not too sure about that information though. Our *Munshi* Kilachand Gupta will be able to guide you there."

Indrajeet nodded, impressed that the Rani knew so much, even if she didn't have the exact details. "If you'll wait here for me, Aunty, let me go and get a few samples of the crop on this field." He didn't wait for her reply before he got out of his car and stepped into the field. He pulled a couple of plants from their roots and stepped out of the field, leaving them on the floor at the back of the car, before returning to the driver's seat.

"Let's go, Aunty." He didn't want to linger. He was sure these were poppy plants, and had taken a couple to have them checked. And if that were the case, it wasn't a good idea to hang around the area. He decided not to tell Rani Hyma Devi anything before he spoke with *Munshi* Kilachand. The first thing he had to do was to find out if they had a license to grow the plant. If he wasn't mistaken, poppy was being grown on at least a hundred acres of the Jadeja land. Without a license, they could be in deep trouble with the law.

It was lunchtime when they returned to the Jadeja palace, which was how Indrajeet had timed it. "You must have lunch here, *Kunwar* Indrajeet." Hyma Devi insisted.

"I will, thank you," said Indrajeet, walking into the hallway. "Let me have a wash first though." He went in the direction of the washroom on the ground floor. Returning after a few minutes, he walked in the direction of the dining room where Hyma Devi was supervising the place setting for two.

"I hope you like chicken curry and *aloo pethe ka saag*," Hyma Devi said as a maidservant brought the dishes out from the kitchen and began to serve.

Indrajeet shrugged. "I like all kinds of food, Aunty. This is fine." He helped himself to the hot *missi rotis* placed in a basket, the wide variety of chutneys and tomato-cucumber slices. He refused to stand on formality despite being the son-in-law of the house.

Hyma Devi glared at him for a minute before looking down at her plate, beginning to eat from it. It was no use feeling irritated. Her daughter's husband was what he was.

They moved to the sitting room to have coffee, Indrajeet having refused the rich desserts on offer. Hyma Devi sat back on her sofa, nursing her cup of coffee in both her hands.

"How old was Yashodhara when she was molested?" Indrajeet dropped the words casually when there was a lull in the conversation, though his gaze was anything but casual.

It was a wonder that Hyma Devi didn't drop her coffee cup from hands which suddenly seemed paralysed. She looked him squarely in the eye, before saying, "What are you talking about?"

"You heard me, Aunty. Just in case you missed it, let me repeat myself. How old was Yashodhara when she was molested?" The expression on his face had become stern.

"You are my son-in-law, *Kunwar* Indrajeet. If it had been someone else, I would have…"

"Just presume for a couple of minutes I'm not your son-in-law, but someone else. What would have been your answer?"

"I'd have had you arrested."

"For what?"

"For slandering my daughter's name."

Indrajeet gave her a keen look, though his voice was mild when he said. "Isn't that an extreme reaction?"

"I don't think so."

He shrugged. "Okay, now I'm asking you the question once again as your son-in-law. What's your answer now?"

The few seconds which elapsed after the shock of hearing the most unexpected question from Yashodhara's husband, helped Hyma Devi recover her poise. She was feeling more prepared to answer him since the shock had worn off. "I'd say that someone has been feeding you with false information." She sat ramrod straight on the sofa, her hands folded on her lap as she looked directly at him while giving him the answer.

"What if I say it was Yashodhara herself who told me?" His voice might have been soft, but it still had the impact of the ring of a loud bell in the silent room.

"I refuse to believe it." Hyma Devi lost her cool as she got up from the sofa and walked a few steps away from him, finding it difficult to hide her anger now.

"You refuse to believe what? That Yashodhara told me or…"

She turned around in a flash. "*Kunwarji,* will you please stop this nonsense? I know for a fact Yashodhara is happy with you and I sincerely hope you are also happy with her as your wife. I don't…"

"We are as happy as the circumstances will let us be. What will you say if I tell you that we haven't as yet consummated our marriage?" Indrajeet dropped his bombshell, feeling a deep urge to shake his mother-in-law's composure.

"What?" Hyma Devi stopped in her tracks, a hand at her throat, her eyes, more brown than green, having gone wide. Her face had blanched, leaving her pale and quavering.

"You heard me."

"You don't mean that." Her voice was a shocked whisper as she continued to stare at him pathetically.

Indrajeet sighed exaggeratedly. "Give me one reason why I would be having this conversation with you if I didn't mean it."

Hyma Devi looked down at her son-in-law, from where she was standing, immense hatred in her eyes. Why the hell did he have to dig into old wounds? Couldn't he just leave things alone? What kind of a man couldn't keep his wife happy in bed? She conveniently refused to acknowledge her fault in swearing Yashodhara to secrecy. Indrajeet couldn't be blamed in any manner whatsoever. Hyma Devi had too much on her plate right now. What with the farmers giving trouble, the crops not giving optimum yield and worst of all, her ex-husband, Jaswantlal Diwekar, to be released from jail in less than six months! Didn't she have enough complications in her life? Why the hell did Yashodhara's husband have to create more?

She cleared her throat, talking slowly as she thought on her feet. "*Kunwarji*, I think you are mistaken. Yashodhara has always been an obedient child. She will never go against your wishes. She…"

"Oh, I know that of course." He gave Hyma Devi a sarcastic smile that never reached his eyes before continuing, "She's so obedient that she refuses to break the promise she made to you, her mother, that she would never speak about what happened to her."

The look of relief on Hyma Devi's face brought Indrajeet to his feet as he walked close to her and stood in front of her, his stance threatening. "Do you care at all for your only child? Yashodhara's suffering, damn it. There's so much pain buried deep within her and she's unable to express it only because her mother, you, have made her swear that she wouldn't speak about it to anyone on earth." His voice had risen by now.

"How dare you?" Hyma Devi snarled. "Do you remember who you are talking to? I am the Rani of Bhatewar. No one speaks to me so disrespectfully and gets away with it." Her face was red with temper now.

"I know only too well who I'm talking to. I'm speaking to a coward who is so worried about the opinion of society that she doesn't care about her daughter's mental health." Indrajeet refused to be cowed down.

"What do you know of anything? Do you know the anguish a single parent undergoes in keeping such a disreputable fact from getting to the ears of people? Do you know how difficult it was to shift along with my only child to another country for the same reason? Do you..."

Indrajeet's eyes went wide with shock. "Are you saying that it happened even before you both moved to England? If that's the case, she must have been barely thirteen when this happened to her. Damn it, Rani Hyma Devi, Yashodhara must have been a child." There was deep anguish in his voice as he glared at his mother-in-law. "Did she tell you what happened?"

Yashodhara had insisted that she had spoken about 'whatever' to no one.

Hyma Devi shook her head. "No. I wouldn't let her put it into words, making it more real than what it was."

"What? Are you saying you didn't let Yashodhara talk to you? What kind of a mother are you? How could you do this to your young daughter?" He turned away abruptly and walked towards the doorway to the sitting room. He never wanted to set eyes on his mother-in-law, ever again. She had shown absolutely no compassion towards her daughter's horrible experience. While Indrajeet still didn't know what had actually happened, he was sure by now that it was something terrible and traumatic. So much so, Hyma Devi had urgently shifted her child as far away as England after extracting a solemn promise that she never ever spoke about it.

His heart burned with such anguish when he thought of the little girl who had not been given an opportunity to overcome the horrors of her past. He was seriously worried he might just throttle Hyma Devi for being a total moron.

He stopped at the doorway and turned to look at his mother-in-law who was standing exactly where he had left her. "One last thing before I go. Will you release your daughter from the stupid promise which you forced her to make?" He waited for her answer, but turned to leave after a few minutes when none was forthcoming.

Hyma Devi walked up and down, wearing a hole in the carpet as she tried to come to a decision. However angry she felt towards her son-in-law, it was obvious he loved his wife. Despite being married for a month and a half, Indrajeet hadn't thought of divorcing his wife even though he still hadn't had a physical relationship with her. And his family obviously didn't know. Otherwise, the *Rajmata* would have drawn and quartered both Yashodhara and Hyma Devi by now. A soft sigh escaped Hyma Devi, a new respect forming in her mind for Prince Indrajeet Thakore.

She needed her son-in-law's help not just in dealing with the farmers. More importantly, Hyma Devi had been hoping to talk to Indrajeet about her ex-husband Jaswantlal, who was going to be released from prison soon. Without telling him the truth, she had hoped to take his help in keeping the man from harming Yashodhara. If anyone could protect her daughter, it would be her son-in-law.

But she couldn't ask for his support if she didn't comply with his wishes now. Hyma Devi wore out the carpet some more by continuously pacing up and down. What was the worst thing which would happen if Yashodhara spoke to her husband about what had happened so long ago? He was obviously not a person to go ratting about it to anyone. She realised that she didn't really have a choice before picking up the phone and calling her daughter's cell.

11

The eleven going on twelve-year-old Yashodhara looked up when she heard her bedroom door open. She was sitting at her work desk completing her maths home-work when she saw Jaswantlal Diwekar, her stepfather, enter the room. She got up with a jerk. *What is he doing here at this time of the night, when Mama isn't home?*

Hyma Devi had left the palace barely an hour ago as she had to attend a charity function. Jaswantlal had told her he was too tired to accompany her. Her mother had married her stepfather about a year ago. Yashodhara had never felt comfortable in his presence, especially when his eyes roved over her from head to toe which happened too often and always when her mother wasn't looking. The sensitive preteen kept her thoughts to herself as she could see that her mother was happy with her new husband. She didn't want to spoil the atmosphere in the house.

But she could never get herself to call her mother's new husband 'Papa' as he had suggested many a time. Yashodhara tried her best not to address him directly, calling him 'Uncle' when she really needed to.

But why the hell was he here now?

She gave him a wary look, doing her best to curtail the fear rising from the depths of her stomach even as he shut the door gently. Yashodhara didn't notice he had pushed the bolt in place.

"Do you want something, Uncle?" asked Yashodhara politely, holding herself stiffly, her arms tucked tightly against her thin body, slouching as she did her best to keep her burgeoning breasts out of his line of vision.

"Yes, my darling stepdaughter. I wanted to spend some time with you. You know, we've never bonded as father and daughter. I think that's because we have never had the time or the privacy. It's been a little more than a year since I married your mother. Isn't it time that we get to know each other? Your mother is out and will take at least another couple of hours to return. Now is the best time."

He walked over and sat on her bed without even a by-your-leave, making Yashodhara quake with temper as well as nerves, making himself comfortable against the silk-covered cushions piled at the bedhead. He patted the space next to him invitingly, saying, "Come along child, and let's have the chat which is long overdue. Would you like me to ask for some tea, perhaps?" He gave her a smile, showing all of his teeth.

Yashodhara's heart was beating like a drum roll, the blood soaring in her brain, filling her ears with a powerful buzz, making her head spin. With a humongous effort, she stiffened her spine and said,

"I have loads of home-work to complete, Uncle. Tomorrow, please?" Her throat was choked, her voice coming out in a rasp as she forced the words out of her parched lips.

"Will you come here of your own volition or would you like me to come there and get you?" Jaswantlal's voice was silky, in direct contrast to the cold venom in his dark eyes.

An inadvertent shudder passed through Yashodhara's slight body as she gave her bedroom door a quick look, calculating the distance between her desk to the door as against the distance between the bed and the door. Would he be able to reach the door before her?

Two thoughts were seriously worrying her. One was the way he had settled himself on her bed without an invitation. She would have to ask the servants to throw away the sheets. And the other was the expression in his eyes. Jaswantlal seemed capable of cruelty. No way was she going to go sit next to him.

Yashodhara decided to flee and rushed to the door and fervently clutched the handle in order to pull it open. It refused to budge and only then did she notice that the big, brass bolt at the top was in place. Before she could reach up to pull it out, she yelled as she felt her stepfather clutch her long hair at the nape of her neck with a heavy hand.

"You little devil. Don't you know better than to disobey your elders?" He thrust his face close to hers, obviously enjoying the expression of terror in her eyes.

Though tall for her age at four feet, eight inches, her stepfather's gigantic figure was still intimidating, especially as he was standing closer to her than he had ever been. Yashodhara glanced up, gasping for breath at the same time, reaching out with both her hands to pull his hand off her hair. Her delicate scalp hurt under his vicious hold and his face was so close to hers she gagged at the smell of stale beer. "Let me go."

"Ask me nicely," he ordered. "Say, 'let me go, Papa'." There was glee in Jaswantlal's face as he pulled her hair even harder.

Yashodhara shook her head, unsuccessfully, tears pouring down her cheeks by now.

Instead of bringing remorse, it only seemed to excite her stepfather all the more. "That's too bad. Since you can't see me as your Papa, I won't look on you as my daughter." He reached out with his free right hand and squeezed one of her breasts, hard.

Yashodhara screamed, trying to jerk away from him, only ending up hurting herself further as he refused to let go. Her nubile and young breasts hurt as he groped both of them, pinching the nipples hard, a maniacal joy on his face as he leered at her, smacking his thick lips.

She stopped screaming and took a deep breath before kicking him on his shin, as hard as it was humanly possible for a twelve-year-old young lady. She sobbed as she harmed herself more than she did him. "Let me go, please." Yashodhara was begging by now, her head throbbing with the way he was jerking her silky locks, his hold painfully relentless.

He let go of her hair suddenly only to lift her up his arms and carry her towards the bed, while she screamed at the top of her voice even as she kicked him wherever she could reach.

Jaswantlal swore as her foot connected with his privates, before dropping her on the bed like a sack of potatoes. "You little bitch! How dare you?" he snarled, lifting a hand to slap her across her face.

Yashodhara was stunned for only a second as she fell back on the bed. But after that fleeting moment, she didn't really know where she found the strength as she rolled across the bed to slide down from the other side, running as far away as she could from the demon who was her stepfather. Jaswantlal pounced to catch hold of her, but missed by a hair's breadth as Yashodhara slid out of his reach, making him roar in temper, making her quake even as she ran, a powerful adrenaline rush giving strength to her trembling legs.

While there were a number of servants in the house, Yashodhara realised that no one would have heard her as the four-hundred-year-old palace walls were too thick. She rushed towards the en suite bathroom, hoping to lock herself in until her mother reached home. She entered the bathroom and shut the door, locking it, leaning against it as she took long breaths, tears streaming down her cheeks. Her scalp felt as if it was on fire while her breasts ached terribly, the nipples throbbing in pain. And she could already feel her left cheek swelling where she had received his slap. Oh, how she hated the man who was her stepfather. She shut her eyes only to open them in a hurry as her mind recalled his demonic expression with absolute clarity.

Yashodhara slid down against the bathroom wall as her legs gave away beneath her. She folded them close to her body before wrapping her arms tightly around her bent legs, burying her face into her knees, sobs wracking through her frail, petite body.

Apparently, the nightmare wasn't over yet it seemed as she heard Jaswantlal banging on the bathroom door with his fists. "Open the door, you cunt, unless you want me to break it down."

She lifted her head to look at the door that had been fitted in recent years and was not as strong as the old ones that came with the original palace. It shuddered under the pressure of Jaswantlal throwing his weight on it before it burst off its hinges to fall back, allowing him to walk in freely.

He turned right and then left and saw her cowering on the floor, her face raised up to pin him with her panicked gaze. He laughed uproariously before taking a couple of strides that brought him close to her. Pulling her up with a rough hand, he tucked a hand into the neck of her nightshirt and pulled hard until it tore from the neckline to the hem, leaving the front of her naked body bared to his burning gaze.

"Noooooooo." Yashodhara's scream fell on deaf ears as a crazed Jaswantlal had his way with her right there on the bathroom floor.

It was more than an hour later when Hyma Devi walked into her daughter's bedroom, to wish her goodnight. She made it a point to spend a few minutes with her only child each night before they went to sleep. Surprised to find the lights off at quarter to ten, she walked to the bed. Yashodhara stayed up till at least eleven in the night, though she spent the late evening closeted in her own room, either studying or reading. Hyma Devi was well aware that her second husband and her daughter didn't get along. With a sigh, she switched on the bedside lamp, sitting down on the bed as she reached out to her sleeping daughter. Only to find the bed empty. Hyma Devi turned towards the bathroom and found the door ajar. Was Yashodhara in there? She got up, calling out, "Yasho?"

Not getting an answer, she walked closer to the bathroom and called again, "Yasho, baby, are you in there?"

Was that the sound of moaning? Hyma Devi went into the bathroom in a half-run, her heart beating loudly as she wondered what could have gone wrong.

For all her anxiety, Hyma Devi was totally unprepared for the sight that met her eyes.

Yashodhara was lying on the floor, her face swollen beyond recognition, her arms crossed over her naked breasts, the torn nightshirt lying beneath her, soaked in blood.

"Yasho!" Hyma Devi went on knees beside the limp figure of her child, touching a gentle hand to her shoulder. "My baby! What happened?" Even as she asked the question, Hyma Devi knew. She just knew what must have happened. She gathered her daughter's prone body in her arms, rocking her gently, tears pouring down her eyes. "Oh my baby, t'is all because of me." Her voice was soft as she cried, continuing to hold her daughter in her arms.

"Mama." Yashodhara called out in a hoarse voice that trembled. "Oh Mama! He hurt me so terribly, Mama. I…"

"Shh, my baby. Don't talk. Let me get you some water to drink first. And yes, a warm bath. That's what you need. Let me fill the bathtub." Hyma Devi placed her daughter back on the floor gently before getting up, a determined expression on her face. The royal queen, who summoned a servant for the smallest of things, personally waited on her daughter that night.

"Mama, please. Listen to me. I, he… your husband…"

"No, don't talk, Yasho. I *know*. You don't need to tell me. There's no need to worry. You won't see Jaswant again. That's my promise to you." Hyma Devi was determined to protect her daughter even if she needed to kill her husband with her bare hands. She ran water in the bathtub before she went out to fetch a bottle of water from the bedside table in Yashodhara's room.

Yashodhara was still in a half daze, not fully aware of what had happened to her. Her body hurt excruciatingly, all over. She drank deeply from the bottle her mother placed against her mouth, wincing as the cuts on her lips opened again, drops of blood trickling down her chin. "Mama, you won't believe what happened. He…"

"Shh. Let me help you up. You're obviously aching all over. You will feel a mite better after a bath."

Yashodhara looked at her mother's face. But Hyma Devi refused to meet her daughter's pathetic gaze. "Let me talk, Mama." Her voice was pleading as she choked on her words. She so wanted to get everything off her chest. Right now, she wasn't even sure if she hated Jaswantlal for what he had done to her or herself for being born the female of the species.

"No, Yasho." Hyma Devi's voice was firm. She gently lifted her daughter to her feet before walking her towards the bath.

Yashodhara winced as she took a step, her feminine core hurting miserably. She bent down to see the blood at the top of her thighs and moaned, sagging against her mother's slender frame. "What has he done to me, Mama?" She did know about the birds and the bees. She also knew about being inappropriately touched. Her mother had taught her about the first and warned her about the next. But… but… she wasn't sure what her stepfather had done to her, except that she knew that he had wounded her dreadfully, not just physically but mentally also.

Hyma Devi patted Yashodhara gently on her shoulder as she heard her daughter groan in pain as she slid into the bathtub and settled down. "Every bone and muscle in my body is aching, Mama."

Not really replying to her daughter, Hyma Devi sat on the bath-stool next to it and said "Listen, Yasho. I'm a queen and you are a princess. What happened to you—yes, I know what exactly happened in here when I was gone—must not be spoken about. I don't want you to talk about it to anyone, not even to me. Do not put it into words as even the walls have ears. The reputation of our royal household is at stake. As I told you before, you'll never have to see Jaswant again. You stay in your room until you're completely healed. I'll take care of you myself. I…"

"But, Mama!" Tears poured down Yashodhara's face as her anxious heart beat heavily. "What happened to me, Mama? What did he do to me?" Her life had been rather protected and Yashodhara had never really understood the meaning of the word rape. She knew that Jaswantlal had hurt her horribly, but still didn't know what he had actually done to her. She had fainted when he had torn her dress and woken up with an excruciating pain in her vagina after some time. This was after he had gotten off her body and was pulling his pants on. Did that mean what she thought it meant?

Yashodhara turned her face to her mother to ask, only to see Hyma Devi shake her head. "No, baby. Don't talk! Just wash away the filth from your body and forget this ever happened."

It was very easy for her mother to say it. How could Yashodhara forget the horror that had taken place?

Hyma Devi never spoke to her second husband after that. She slept in her daughter's bedroom that night and called the commissioner of police the first thing next morning. "Hello Bhupinder. I need a favour." She explained that she wanted Jaswantlal Diwekar to be arrested for theft and forgery. "I don't really care how you manage it. But he has to get a life term."

"Isn't that the man you are married to, Rani Hyma Devi?" Bhupinder wanted to be sure he had heard her right. Long ago, she had used her influence to help Bhupinder rise up through the police ranks. Now, the commissioner was only too eager to return the favour.

"That's right. But not for long! I'll file for a divorce the minute you arrest him. And you'd better get it done ASAP, Commissioner." There was a note of authority in her voice. Not for nothing was Hyma Devi a queen, even in this democratic age.

Jaswantlal didn't know what hit him. He had been sure his stepdaughter would be too ashamed and afraid to talk about what had happened to her. What he hadn't expected was to be handcuffed the moment he got off the breakfast table the very next morning.

Things moved fast as evidence piled up against him and soon, Jaswantlal found himself in jail, serving a term of fourteen years for three different offences.

The newspapers had written a couple of articles about the queen's second husband being arrested and the subsequent filing for divorce. But it wasn't that big a news for them to pursue it since Jaswantlal Diwekar was just an ordinary man. Hyma Devi had issued a press release regarding the same and it put an end to all the gossip.

Hyma Devi refused to leave her daughter alone even with the servants. What if the young girl mentioned something to any of them in a moment of weakness? No, she intended to keep the whole incident a secret. The world must not know that the young Jadeja princess had been raped by her stepfather.

Hyma Devi had made her daughter swallow a pill the morning after the incident, just to ensure there was no chance of an accidental pregnancy. After that, she took care of her day and night, refusing to take help from the many servants who worked in the palace. Yashodhara was completely taken aback by her mother's behaviour. The queen was used to being waited upon hand and foot, every moment of her waking hours. However, Hyma Devi took care of Yashodhara who was incarcerated in her room till the last bruise had disappeared from her body.

Hyma Devi wouldn't allow Yashodhara to talk about her traumatic experience. The child burned with the need for it. She felt so anguished that one day, in a fit of frustration, she took a pair of scissors and chopped off her long hair, the hair that Jaswant had fisted in his hand to keep her in his control. Yashodhara cut it off as close to her scalp as possible and almost smiled when she saw her image in the full-length mirror in her bedroom. Only the smile disappeared after a few seconds as the horrific memories took over once again.

That evening, Hyma Devi let out a shriek when she set eyes on her daughter. "Yasho, what have you done to yourself?"

Yashodhara gave her mother a wan smile. "Nothing, Mama. Just gave myself a new look." She didn't owe her mother any explanation. Hyma Devi didn't want to hear about what had actually happened that night during her absence. Why should Yashodhara give her a reason for chopping off her hair?

"Oh, Yasho." Hyma Devi hugged her daughter, her throat choking with anguish. Would her daughter ever be able to lead a normal life? It would be difficult for Yashodhara to return to school as if nothing had happened. And what if she said something to any of her close friends? Word would spread around like wildfire and the reputation of the Jadejas would be in shreds. That's when she came up with a plan.

Yashodhara protested loudly two days later, when her mother insisted that the two of them move to England where she had procured a seat for her daughter at one of the exclusive private schools. "Mama, all my friends are here. I don't want to go."

A month had gone by and her body had healed, and she had trained herself to bury her trauma deep within the recesses of her mind, completely unaware that it was still a festering wound. Her pain rose to the fore when her mother told her that they were shifting to England. Yashodhara hadn't even had a chance to speak to her best friend, Chitrangada, for the last one month. Her friend called up many times but it was always Hyma Devi who answered the phone. She had already spread the word about Yashodhara being down with a severe form of chicken-pox.

Hyma Devi replied, "Listen, Yasho. It's best we move to England for a few years. The new environment will help you forget whatever happened here."

"But Mama. Let me at least talk to Chitra. I haven't spoken to her since... since that horrible night. She's my best friend, Mama. You know that." Yashodhara refused to let the tears fall from her shimmering hazel green eyes. No, there was nothing to cry about. Her mother had told her to forget the incident as a bad dream. How Yashodhara wished she could do just that! The scene in her bedroom and then the bathroom kept coming to the fore every time she had a couple of minutes to herself. So much so, Yashodhara had become scared of being alone. In a way she was glad her mother spent a lot of time with her these days as it left her with very little time to think.

Now, Hyma Devi said, "Listen, Yasho. I need you to promise me something. Promise me that you will never, ever, talk about what happened to you that night, to any living soul. The world is unkind, my baby. They will treat you terribly if they get to know."

Yashodhara looked at her mother's face, her innocent eyes wary. Should she feel ashamed about it? But then, why? She had done nothing. It wasn't her fault that Jaswantlal had behaved the way he had. Why should she not talk about it? Yashodhara wanted to scream from the roof of the palace, to anyone who would listen, about the way she had been abused. People should know, especially young girls like herself. They should know that there were evil men out there, who could harm them. But her mother wouldn't let her tell even Chitrangada about it.

"Mama, please. I need to talk to someone." She rubbed her aching chest, unable to ease the pain in her heart. "I feel so heavy inside, keeping the pain and trauma buried within. It hurts, Mama."

Hyma Devi hugged her, kissing her on her forehead. "I know, Yasho, I know. That's exactly why I'm saying that we should move away from here. Not forever. Just for a few years until everything blows over. You will recover faster that way. I am your mother. I know what's best for you."

But no, even as Yashodhara tried her best to push the pain deep within, it continued to gnaw at her innards, the misery refusing to fade over time, not like her mother had promised her it would.

12

Tears were pouring unchecked down Yashodhara's cheeks as she finished telling her husband about what had happened all those years ago. The pain and anguish seemed to gush like a fountain from deep within her gut as she spoke about the way her stepfather had abused her that evening, for the very first time since almost fourteen years.

"I'm sorry Jeet. I feel so ashamed that you are saddled with me, a tarnished princess. You surely deserve better."

She had been sitting across him as she spoke to him, refusing his offer of holding her in his arms. But Indrajeet couldn't be put off any longer as he got up to lift her bodily and gently seated her on his lap, his arms around her. He had wanted to cry along with her as he heard her talk to him about her traumatic experience. He held back his tears with great difficulty since he was scared to further upset a trembling and quavering Yashodhara.

He held her close to his heart, his hand caressing her back soothingly. "I'm sorry that I wasn't there for you when this happened to you, my sweetheart. How

I wish I could have protected you!" He hid his temper well, angrier with Yashodhara's mother than the scum who had actually molested her. Yashodhara had been holding all this hurt and pain inside her, not speaking about it to any living soul, not until her mother had called her to release her from her promise. What kind of a woman was Hyma Devi, if the opinions of a so-called aristocratic society mattered more to her than her daughter's unrelieved trauma?

Yashodhara lifted her face from where it was burrowed in his chest and looked up at him, surprise in her gaze. "Don't you feel ashamed of me? Of being associated with me?" Of course, he must be. He wasn't telling her only because she was too upset just now.

"Why would I do that, Yash? It wasn't your fault your stepfather did what he did. Why should I be ashamed of you? I adore you, my sweetheart."

Her hazel green eyes had dried up but grew wet again on hearing his words. "I love you too, Jeet. Do you really think we could ever lead a normal life?" There was yearning in her tremulous voice.

"I don't just believe we will have a normal life. I promise you we will. Come now. Have a wash. I'll take you out for a long drive and dinner. Would you like that?" She needed a change of scene, a breather to digest the fact that her shameful secret was neither shameful nor a secret any more.

Yashodhara smiled through her tears, looking at her husband adoringly. "I'd love that."

"That's my princess."

They got out of the Thakore palace in half an hour, Indrajeet taking her for a long drive as promised. "Have you been to Maharaja International?" She probably hadn't since Yashodhara had returned from England fairly recently. Moreover, she didn't go out much, as she intensely disliked being in the company of men.

She turned in her seat to look at him, shaking her head. "What's that?"

"It's a five-star hotel owned by my friend Ritvik Bansal. He bought our summer palace and converted it into a heritage hotel."

"Sounds awesome. I'd love to see it." While she tried to sound enthusiastic, there was a deep sadness lurking in her eyes.

"Perfect. Let's go. Ritvik is married to Sia who runs the beauty salon at his hotel. They have two kids, Aarya and Akshat. And at least a dozen cats the last time I saw."

"What? A dozen? Do they run a cat farm or something?"

There was astonishment on her face as she smiled at Indrajeet, exactly what he had been hoping for. Indrajeet laughed. "Let's go ask them," he said, as he drove through the tall gates of Maharaja International.

"It's a beautiful hotel," exclaimed Yashodhara after she got out of the car and looked up at the five-storied building.

"Isn't it?!" Indrajeet took her hand in his and guided her into the reception.

"Hello Jeet." Akhil Shetty, the Front Office Manager of the hotel came out from behind the reception counter to greet Indrajeet, with a wide smile on his face. "How are you?"

Indrajeet grinned back at Akhil. "I'm doing very well, thank you, Akhil. This is my wife…"

"Princess Yashodhara. How can I forget the lovely princess?! Welcome to Maharaja International, ma'am. I am Akhil Shetty, the front office manager." Akhil turned to greet her.

With her eyes focussed on the floor, Yashodhara replied, "Hello Mr Shetty. And thank you."

"Is Ritvik around?" Indrajeet asked.

"In his office. Let me ping him." Akhil moved towards the reception to call his boss on the intercom.

"Don't bother if he's busy." Indrajeet was insistent.

"Ritvik's never too busy for you, Jeet." Speaking softly into the phone, Akhil said, "Ritvik, Jeet and Princess Yashodhara are here. Shall I…? Okay, will do." He kept the receiver back and said to Indrajeet, "Please go on to Ritvik's office. He's never too busy for you, as I said."

"Thanks, Akhil. Come along, Yash. Let's go to Ritvik's office first."

Yashodhara looked around, taking in the opulent surroundings as they walked hand-in-hand, to the far end of the reception. Indrajeet knocked on a door before entering. "Hey."

"Hey buddy!" Ritvik Bansal, the CEO of Maharaja International, got up from his swivel chair behind a large work desk and walked forward to greet his friend. "I'm so glad to see you." He hugged Indrajeet before turning to Yashodhara. "Hello, Princess. Welcome to my hotel."

"Hello." Yashodhara's voice was soft as she greeted her husband's friend, even as she looked down at the massive rosewood desk that took centre place in the office.

"I'm not sure if you remember meeting him at our wedding, Yash. This is Ritvik Bansal, a close friend."

Yashodhara nodded, her head still bent low.

"Why don't you both sit down and let me order something to drink. Your usual, Jeet?" When Indrajeet nodded, Ritvik turned to Yashodhara and asked, "And you, princess, what would you like to drink?"

"Some fresh fruit juice, please."

Ritvik nodded, giving Indrajeet an enquiring look, a dark eyebrow up, to ask if everything was alright. Indrajeet shrugged, giving his friend an imperceptible nod.

Ritvik placed the orders and turned to look at his guests. "I would like you both to come home with me. We can order food from any of the restaurants here. But I am sure Sia would love to entertain you at home. Unless you guys are keen to dine here, privately?

What say, Jeet? Better still, princess, what would you like to do?"

"I'd love to go to your house and meet your wife and kids." There was no hesitation in Yashodhara's voice even if she still refused to look Ritvik in his eyes.

"Great. We'll have our drinks and move to my cottage. Give me a sec!" He opened his cell to call Sia and let her know he was bringing guests. "No honey, I'm not going to tell you who they are. You're in for a surprise." There was laughter in Ritvik's voice when he spoke to his wife.

"So, how's life, man? Being married obviously suits you." Ritvik grinned at Indrajeet. "You are glowing."

Yashodhara turned to look in fascination at her husband when she heard him laugh. Was it true? Was Indrajeet really happy married to her? But how could he be? She hadn't given him any cause for happiness.

But Indrajeet was grinning back at his friend as if his married life couldn't be better. And he appeared genuine too. In the weeks she had been with her husband, Yashodhara had noticed that there were no pretentious airs surrounding him. He always meant what he said and was cheerful all the time. Her throat felt choked when she realised that he must truly love her. Would she ever be in a position to deserve so much love?

A waiter walked in with a tray carrying their drinks. Yashodhara took her glass of mixed fruit juice and sipped on it, listening to the two men chat.

"So, Yashodhara, is Jeet treating you well? You can tell me the truth." There was laughter in Ritvik's voice as he clanked his glass of whiskey on the rocks with Jeet's glass of the same.

Yashodhara's smile was small as she continued to gaze at the desk. "Jeet is marvellous towards me. I'm the one who is constantly giving him trouble."

Ritvik was startled as he looked from one to the other of his unexpected guests, shaking his head slowly. He looked again at his friend, an eyebrow up in enquiry.

Indrajeet laughed. "I love Yash, exactly the way she is." He didn't notice the colour suffusing his wife's cheeks as he addressed their host.

They chatted some more as they finished their drinks. "Shall we go?" Ritvik got up from his chair. "Sia must be dying of curiosity by now."

They walked out of the hotel from the back door and walked towards the sprawling structure that Ritvik called 'cottage'.

The door opened even before they were halfway to his home when two tornados hurled themselves at Ritvik, yelling, "Daddyyyyy."

Laughing, Ritvik bent down and lifted both his children into his arms as Aarya and Akshat clung to his neck from both sides, kissing him soundly on both his cheeks. Anyone looking at the way they greeted him, couldn't be mistaken for believing that they hadn't set eyes on their father in months instead of the few hours since lunchtime.

He let them down before saying, "Say 'hello' to Jeet uncle and Princess Yashodhara. Princess, meet my daughter Aarya and my son Akshat."

Thrilled as she eyed the children, Yashodhara went down on her knees to greet them. "Hello Aarya," she said, shaking the chirpy six-year-old girl's hand before turning to greet the two-year-old boy. "Hello Akshat."

"I'm daddy's princess," Aarya declared in a clear voice, eyeing the tall woman in front of her.

Yashodhara grinned. "I'm sure you are, Princess Aarya."

"Are you also your daddy's princess?" Aarya's silver eyes glowed with curiosity.

Yashodhara laughed. "Not really. And you can call me Yasho Aunty."

"'Ello, Yaso Aunthie." Akshat greeted her in a lisping voice, raising his arms to be lifted.

Surprised and thrilled, Yashodhara stood up to lift the little boy in her arms and was touched when he gave her a sound kiss on her cheek.

"Akshat sure has his father's instincts of a lady-killer." Indrajeet laughed as he teased Ritvik in a near whisper. Both the kids had sharp hearing and tended to catch on to phrases definitely not meant for their little ears.

"Shuddup, Jeet." Ritvik laughed too as they walked the last few steps which brought them to the wide-open front door of his cottage.

Indrajeet held Aarya's hand as she told him about the horse-riding event where she had won a first prize. "I'll show you the cup I got, Jeet Uncle."

"Sure, my pet. I can't wait to see it."

"Hello, Jeet." Sia had walked to the door just then and greeted Indrajeet like a long-lost friend. "I'm so glad you finally decided to visit us along with your wife. I've been telling Ritvik to invite you. Only he insists you both need your privacy. I…"

"Well, I didn't want to socialise for at least six months after I got married to this lady here." Ritvik caught Sia in his arms and gave her a kiss on her lips. "And that's why I thought of leaving you newlyweds alone. I wasn't wrong, was I?"

Sia gave her husband a mock glare before turning to Yashodhara. "Hello Princess. Welcome to our home. I'm Sia, wife to this Neanderthal. Welcome to our home."

"Hello Sia. Please call me Yasho. You have such lovely kids."

Sia smiled warmly at Yashodhara before taking the protesting Akshat from her arms and leaving him down. "Let Yasho Aunty sit down, Akshat. You can show her your toys later."

Akshat took off at a run, excited to show his toys to their new guests.

Yashodhara was not just fascinated with the children but also the closeness between Ritvik and Sia. They touched each other at every opportunity while she caught their eyes connecting together fairly often. They must have been married for at least seven years or more, she guessed. They seemed so much in love.

Yashodhara smothered the sigh that rose from deep within her being. Would she and Indrajeet ever achieve a similar level of closeness and camaraderie? She turned to look at her husband who took her hand in his as if he sensed her uneasiness.

Ritvik walked to the bar at one end of the hall and Indrajeet got up to follow him. "Is something the problem, bro?" Ritvik asked his friend outright. "I can see that you're happy, but your wife isn't."

Indrajeet sighed, tucking his hands into the pockets of his jeans. "I love Yash, as I said before. And she loves me too." He sighed, realising why he had opted to visit Ritvik today. They had become really close since the time Ritvik had shifted to Udaipur seven years ago. "There are issues, though." He looked up into his friend's dark eyes. "She was raped when she was barely twelve." The words seemed to burst forth from Indrajeet's lips as he poured out his anguish to his best friend. How he wished he could take away her pain! "The worst part is she wasn't allowed to speak about it to anyone and she's terrified of a physical relationship."

"Ouch!" Ritvik threw an arm around Indrajeet's shoulders. Now he realised why his friend's wife never looked directly into his eyes whenever she addressed him or vice versa. "That must have been a horrible experience made a million times worse by not talking about it." He frowned. "But her mother, was the princess too ashamed to speak with Rani Hyma Devi?"

Indrajeet's expression turned grim. "That's the main issue. Her mother had guessed what had happened. It was Yash's stepfather who had molested her. But Hyma Devi insisted Yash should never speak about it. She…"

"What the fuck!" Ritvik was furious. "How will she heal if she doesn't speak about it? Listen, I've never told you this. But Sia was married before we met. And she left the marriage because she was regularly abused by her father-in-law."

Indrajeet's jaw dropped. "Oh my God!" He turned around to look at his hostess. Sia was on the floor with the kids and Yashodhara had also joined them as a toy train chugged its way around that side of the living room, with four kittens ensconced in the carriages that had their tops open. "But… but looking at Sia, no one would have guessed it. She's so confident and cheerful." He turned back to address Ritvik.

Ritvik poured a measure of whiskey into a crystal glass as he grimaced. "It was a lot of work, but she has finally arrived there. I must say she's one brave lady. It was also lucky that she had help. Kamini Sachdev is a social worker based in Jhunjunu. She took Sia under her wing and ensured she had therapy sessions with a psychiatrist. It's what you should do. Get Yashodhara to speak with a therapist. Would you like me to get you some contacts?"

"Could you do that? It would really be a great help. Better yet, do you mind sharing Kamini Sachdev's contact details? I'd rather Yash went for therapy somewhere away from Udaipur. You heard about her mother's attitude towards this issue. And then there's Grandma. I don't want her throwing a tantrum and turning the healing process on its head."

"I know what you mean. Let me message you Kamini ma'am's contact details right now." Ritvik took his phone out and did just that before continuing, "You can take my name and Sia's too. And Jeet, after the therapy, encourage Yashodhara to talk openly about her experience. The trauma is multiplied when bottled up. Once it's out in the open, the healing is faster. Sia used to think there was something wrong with her and that's why the bastard had done what he had. It took a lot of time and encouragement for her to realise it was no fault of hers."

Indrajeet nodded, his brown eyes shimmering with the pain he was experiencing on his wife's behalf. "Exactly. And that's the reason why I'm so angry with Yash's mother. She has allowed the wound to fester for all these years by making Yash promise never to talk about her traumatic experience and subsequent pain." A ferocious scowl gathered on his forehead as he looked at Ritvik.

"I know what you mean. But then, how did your wife open up?" It wasn't out of idle curiosity Ritvik asked this question as he was genuinely concerned for this charming couple. And Indrajeet was one of his dearest friends.

Indrajeet grinned, his eyes turning mischievous. "I threatened Hyma Devi, quite severely too. I cornered her into giving permission to Yashodhara to break her promise."

Ritvik laughed. "Rani Hyma Devi seems to be the *Rajmata's* twin."

"You said it." Indrajeet nodded, taking his whiskey heavily diluted with soda and ice from Ritvik as he was aware of the drive back home.

The two of them walked towards the other end of the living room where their wives were playing with the children and joined the melee.

It was almost midnight when the royal couple took their leave, promising to visit again soon. "You must come home for dinner soon, Ritvik, Sia." Indrajeet invited them over to their palace.

"Yes, please. And bring Aarya and Akshat too." Yashodhara smiled at her new friend.

"We'll do that."

"Did you enjoy meeting my friends?" Indrajeet turned to look at his wife as he pulled the seat belt across his torso and clicked it in place.

"Loved it. Thank you for bringing me Jeet. I liked Sia. And their kids are adorable." Yashodhara's green eyes shone brightly in the light of the dashboard.

Indrajeet took his wife's hand in his, saying, "I'm so glad. Let's go to Sia's salon tomorrow. I'm sure you'd enjoy a massage or a facial."

Yashodhara's face darkened while the light left her eyes as she slowly shook her head. She didn't want strangers touching her. "Not for me. Let me not stop you."

"Yash." Indrajeet took her chin in his hand, and looked deeply into her eyes. "I'm sorry. Just forget I asked."

Yashodhara blinked her eyelids rapidly, making an effort to quell the tears springing into her eyes. No, she would not cry. She had had a wonderful evening. But… but… a deep sigh shuddered through her body. She would never find the comfort level with her husband—the kind Sia shared with Ritvik.

Indrajeet took his father and mother into confidence, not delving too deeply into details. "I'm taking Yashodhara to Mumbai for a couple of months, Mama. I have taken an appointment with Dr Nalini Singh, a psychiatrist highly recommended by the social worker I told you about. Yashodhara might have to undergo multiple sessions of therapy is what I am told. I don't need to tell you people not to utter a word to Grandma."

Both Gajendar and Ragini nodded their heads vigorously while the later had a worried frown on her face. "I have heard about hypnotherapy. Do you think it's safe, Jeet?" Ragini asked him outright.

Indrajeet hugged his mother, reassuring her. "Don't worry, Mama. Kamini Sachdev recommends the doctor highly. And she also advocates hypnotherapy as it's the one thing which can definitely uproot the trauma deeply embedded within a person's psyche."

Ragini nodded. "Poor Yasho. She must be suffering so much."

Gajendar agreed. "So true. The poor child. No wonder she isn't comfortable around me. I did wonder about it."

Indrajeet said, "Yes, Papa. Now you know why. I'm hoping to get her cured of all that. So, we are leaving first thing tomorrow morning. If Grandma asks, I am off for a business deal and will return when it's signed and sealed. I don't plan to tell her I won't be around for a minimum of two months."

"That's right. You go on Jeet, and don't worry about anything. The hostel, the palace and farms are being managed superbly. I must congratulate you on the processes you have set in place. Everything flows smoothly even when you aren't around."

Indrajeet grinned. "Don't they?! I must say I feel good about it."

Yashodhara and Indrajeet caught an early morning flight to Mumbai and moved directly into a service apartment at Powai which had been hired for a period of two months. It wasn't far from where Dr Nalini Singh lived and practiced at Hiranandani Gardens in Powai.

The royal couple arrived at *Athena*, the building where the doctor lived and ran her clinic, five minutes before the appointment time at 4 pm. The receptionist showed them into the hall. "Please sit down, sir, ma'am. Dr Singh should be with you in a minute."

The doctor entered the hall even as the man completed his sentence, saying, "Hello, Prince and Princess Thakore, right?" She smiled, looking at the young couple as the man nodded. "Please sit down." She pointed to the visitors' chairs before settling down behind her work desk.

"Hello, Dr Singh. Please feel free to call us Jeet and Yasho."

Nalini nodded. "Sure. Would you like some tea or coffee, Yasho and Jeet?"

Once the coffee was served, they continued with their conversation. "Do you want me to wait elsewhere?" Indrajeet asked his wife.

Yashodhara caught his hand in hers, shaking her head. "Please stay with me." She turned to the psychiatrist and said, "If that's okay with you, doctor?"

Nalini nodded her head once again. "Whatever works for you, Yasho." She took a note pad and made notes as she asked the princess many questions regarding her age, her education, her parents, her background and then more subtle questions related to her moods and her emotions.

"Your full name?"

"Princess Yashodhara Jadeja Thakore."

"How old are you?"

"Twenty-four years and eight months."

"Can you tell me something about your education?"

"I studied in Udaipur till seventh standard. Actually, I didn't quite complete the year before I moved to Sussex in England. I did my A-levels and my graduation there. I also have done a few short-term courses to help run my properties."

"So, when did you return to India?"

"A little more than two years ago."

"How many people are there in your family? I mean both before and after you got married." The doctor knew from Indrajeet that they had been married for six weeks.

"Before marrying Jeet, I used to live with my mother, Rani Hyma Devi, at our palace in Bhatewar. There are a horde of servants who live in and around the palace. And after marriage, there's my husband, Indrajeet, his grandmother and his parents. We all live in the Thakore palace at Udaipur."

Nalini smiled. "I am honoured to be visited by true blue-blooded royalty."

Yashodhara turned red on hearing that. "There's nothing special about us, doctor. We are no different from the other citizens of our country."

Nalini's smile turned into a grin as she kept her opinion to herself—that Indrajeet and Yashodhara, beginning with their names, their attire and their attitude, couldn't be further removed from regular citizens. More so in the case of Princess Yashodhara. She continued to ask Yashodhara a number of questions to get a thorough idea about her background.

"Okay, now that we have your background all set, I'd like to meet you tomorrow to know more about your habits, your interaction with men and other social skills. Could you come in the morning, at eleven?"

Yashodhara turned to look at her husband before saying, "Sure, doctor, we'll be here."

"Well, from tomorrow the sessions will have to be one-on-one, Yasho. It's better that way." The doctor looked at her patient and her husband alternately.

"I agree," said Indrajeet. "I'll come along with Yash and leave her here with you. I can pick her up later."

"Perfect." The doctor got up from her chair to shake hands with the couple before seeing them out.

"But, Jeet. I don't want to be alone. Why can't you be there with me? It worked alright today." Yashodhara looked at her husband appealingly as they sat across each other in a coffee shop.

Indrajeet smiled at his wife, holding her hand in his. "Listen, sweetheart. You met the doctor. Isn't she nice? Or do you feel uncomfortable?" His brown eyes gazed deeply into her troubled hazel green ones.

"Nalini Singh is nice, definitely. But how do I bare my soul to a stranger?" There was an accusing look on Yashodhara's face as she glared at her husband, feeling as if he was abandoning her.

"Sometimes, Yash, it's easier to speak to a stranger. And also, the doctor knows what works best for you. It isn't as if I don't want to be around. We need to trust Dr Nalini and all her decisions. I just want you to be relieved of this tremendous burden you are carrying."

"Jeet..." Yashodhara placed her head on his shoulder as he threw an arm around her waist and pulled her close. Her voice was choked with emotion.

If it wasn't for her husband, she wouldn't even have taken the first step to get treated. But again, she had been living with this pain for almost fourteen years. The dull ache had become an inherent part of her being. It hadn't been too difficult talking to her husband about it. Even then, she had only shared the basic details with him.

Now, she was scared of what might happen if everything was brought to the fore, all those horrible thoughts and emotions which had been buried deep within. What if it broke her completely?

"I'm scared Jeet. Can't we just forget it happened? I have lived with it all these years and managed to survive. What do you think is going to happen now if I talk to the doctor? She can't go back in time and change what happened, can she?" Her expression was pathetic as Yashodhara appealed to her husband.

"My sweetheart, Dr Nalini Singh will take you through the process of hypnosis and remove all the pain that's deeply buried in your psyche. She'll also help you overcome your fear of men. You must be aware that not all men are bad. You…"

Yashodhara lifted her head from his shoulder to look at Indrajeet's face, a smile on her own. "I know that. You, for one, are the best guy on earth." She hesitated before pressing her lips to his cheek in a tentative kiss.

Hot colour rushed up Indrajeet's rugged face, his brown eyes glowing brightly. "Thanks." He tapped her nose playfully. "Not just me. Just because of a handful of horrible men, it doesn't mean the entire male population except your husband, are nasty human beings."

She smiled. "I might not have agreed before. But now that I know you, I have to admit you're right."

"But you still aren't comfortable in the company of men. You…"

Yashodhara sighed. "What does it matter?" Her mouth was set mutinously. She didn't care for men, period. She was happy with her husband and that was enough for her.

"It does. Every time you refuse to look into a man's eyes and say what you think, you admit to your weakness. It doesn't matter when you are in my father's or Rajvardhan's presence. Not even when you meet Ritvik or Akhil Shetty. But what will happen when you want to deal with your farmers? I know I will always be there for you. But don't you want to be independent?"

Yashodhara looked into her husband's eyes, a slow fire burning in her own. He was right. She would prefer to be independent. And he was right about her refusing to meet men's eyes. That was because she was scared of what she would see there. She so remembered the lustful expression in her stepfather's gaze from that night. She shuddered now as she recalled his leery gaze with crystal clarity, as if it had happened only last night. That was why she could never make eye contact with any man.

Indrajeet had given her no choice and had drawn her out of her shell. And, well, she had only seen gentleness, love and compassion in his gentle brown gaze. Other than that, she had seen the anger and anguish he felt on her behalf and these had only succeeded in empowering her.

She slowly nodded her head now. "You are right, Jeet. I need my independence."

"And," his voice was a soft growl now, "I want you to want me physically, Yash. This trauma is a major block between us. While I'll never force myself on you, I can't wait for the day when you want to make love to me." His eyes had gone soft and appealing as they looked deeply into hers.

"I'm sorry, Jeet. I was being selfish. I..." She stopped when Indrajeet placed a hand on her mouth, effectively stopping her from saying anything further.

He shook his head. "Stop apologising. It's no fault of yours. This is the one thing you need to be clear about."

Yashodhara teared up. "Are you sure? Are you sure I wasn't sending out some kind of a signal which made him behave the way he did?"

Indrajeet got up suddenly, realising the coffee shop was not the right place for this discussion. He took her hand in his and pulled her up. "Let's go and continue this conversation at home."

They took an OLA which dropped them at the gates of Lakeside Chalet by Marriott Executive

Apartments, where they were staying. They took the elevator to the seventh floor and entered apartment number 706.

Indrajeet picked up from where they had left off, the moment he shut the door. "Yash, you need to stop blaming yourself. Your stepfather was a scumbag which is why he did what he did. It was absolutely no fault of yours. Do you hear me?" His hands were on her shoulders as he looked into her eyes, his own brown gaze intense.

"Tch." Yashodhara pulled her gaze from his to stare at his throat; fascinated by the way it worked. "How can you be sure?"

"You are right. I can't be."

Yashodhara lifted her shocked gaze and looked into his. She hadn't expected him to agree to her, not so blatantly. "Eh?"

Indrajeet grinned. "That got your attention, right? Sweetheart, how much ever I try to convince you, you'll only continue to doubt yourself. And that's exactly what I proved to you just now. And that's also exactly the reason why you need to undergo the therapy sessions with Nalini Singh."

Yashodhara nodded her head, slowly. "And Jeet…" She hugged him, her arms going around his trim waist as she spoke softly into his ear. "I want to make love to you too."

14

Kilachand Gupta, *munshi* of the Jadejas, walked swiftly across the path dividing the two fields and reached the small hut-like structure serving as Amarchand Khatri's office. He pushed opened the wooden door and walked in to see a haze of smoke. He tutted in annoyance, calling out, "Amarchand, are you in there somewhere?"

"Gupta*ji*, come on in. I'm sitting in my usual chair," called out the gruff voice of Khatri, the young leader of the new generation of farmers who were keen to make quick money and didn't care if their activities were illegal.

With a heavy frown on his lined face, Kilachand walked warily through the smoke, finding his way through the many rickety stools and chairs occupying the space. He found Khatri right at the back, where the man had said he was seated. The *munshi* ignored the three other men present in the room, his focus only on their leader.

"Are you even aware of the trouble you people are in?" He shook his head before continuing, "I don't think so. Otherwise, Khatri, you wouldn't be sitting back and enjoying your poisonous smoke if you know what is actually happening."

"You sit down Guptaji, and stop being a worry wart. *Koyi kuch nahi bigaad sakta hai.* Do you want to have a smoke?" Khatri laughed loudly before making the offer, as he inhaled more of the heroin smoke from his hand-rolled cigarette.

"*Arre baba*, don't be silly. You very well know that I don't smoke that stupid drug. And are you absolutely certain no one can spoil your business? Let me tell you there is someone who's already working on it. Where were you idiots five days ago, in the afternoon?"

Amarchand Khatri turned and looked at his henchmen before eyeing Kilachand balefully. "Why, what happened?" He must have been at home, fast asleep after a busy morning.

"Rani Hyma Devi's son-in-law, Prince Indrajeet Thakore, had been to your fields and taken samples of the plants there." There was arrogance in Kilachand's voice—as he was the messenger carrying terrible news—as it was obvious the other man didn't have a clue.

"Shit! Are you serious?" Amarchand got up from his chair with a jerk.

"Yes. He asked me if we had a license to produce poppy."

"And what did you tell him?"

"I said, 'YES', of course, you fool. What else could I say when he confronted me with sample plants from this very field? But you know the truth." They had license to produce poppy in ten acres, not the one hundred and fifty acres where it had actually been planted. Kilachand had conveniently not mentioned the statistics to the Thakore prince.

"I think you are jumping the gun, Gupta*ji*. What's the need to panic?"

"You uneducated idiot!" Kilachand's voice vehemently accused Khatri. "What kind of a question is that? Do you know anything about the Thakore prince?"

Amarchand lost his cool as he walked swiftly towards the older man and stood in front of him, toe-to-toe. "I don't know anything about this fancy *phoren*-returned English-speaking prince, nor do I care. These young men who study abroad are basically weaklings who return with nonsensical ideas filling their heads. They are no match for us *desi* people. I'll just rip him apart with my bare hands." Amarchand was so proud of his brawny physique which was way superior to his peanut brain. While he was the one who ran the drug cartel, the brain behind it was a politician. Amarchand was just a local *gunda* who was excellent at throwing his weight around and getting the farmers to do the work. The *munshi* was the intermediary and also the one who maintained — played around with in reality — the account books of the Jadeja farms.

Kilachand glared at the other man. "You will rip apart the prince and do you know what will happen? You'll find your ass in jail within the hour."

Amarchand laughed. "So, do you even realise MLA Hirji will ensure I am bailed out immediately? What are you panicking for?"

Kilachand shook his head. "I always knew you were an idiot. Don't even think life is that easy. Indrajeet Thakore is not just a prince for namesake. He has done so much for the society and he has got powerful connections in the government. He also has friends in the police force. Don't take him lightly, for God's sake."

A deep frown gathered on Amarchand's forehead. "What exactly do you want me to do now?"

"Tighten the security around the fields where poppy is being grown illegally. Better still, harvest them at the earliest and replant some other crop," Kilachand commanded.

"But how can I do that? We'll lose a lot of money that way," Amarchand protested.

"What's more important? Losing some money now or losing the whole business?" Kilachand was highly sarcastic.

"I think you're overreacting. Anyway, there are still a couple of months to go before the harvest. I can't do much before that."

Kilachand glared at Amarchand as if it was all the other man's fault. It would be best to contact MLA Hirji and tell him to use his power to deal with the issue. "Alright then, just make sure there's enough security, that someone is watching the fields round the clock. Let me see what can be done."

"*Theek hai* Guptaji. I'll make sure my men are around day and night."

Kilachand Gupta turned around in a huff to push open the door from inside Amarchand's den and was startled to see a gigantic man standing right outside, almost as if he had been listening to the conversation inside.

"Who are you?" asked Kilachand, his voice and expression stern. "And what are you doing here?"

"I'm a labourer, looking for work. I was told I should meet the leader of the farmers here in this office." The giant answered respectfully. "Are you Amarchand Khatri, sir?"

"What's your name?" Kilachand asked, without answering the other man.

"Meghnath. I'm married and have four kids, all of them small. I need a job desperately to keep them fed and clothed." Meghnath's voice was pleading.

"Come inside." The *munshi* had just realised that he was conducting the conversation on the doorstep and felt rather silly. He turned inwards and called out, "Amarchand, there's a man here who needs a job."

Amarchand spoke to Meghnath for a few minutes and decided to hire him once he realised how strong he was. And this man was also ready to work night shifts, which was most welcome under the circumstances.

If they were even a little smarter, Kilachand and Amarchand would have had the sense to dig deeply before hiring an unknown man. And then only would they have found out that Meghnath was *Rajmata* Santhini Devi's bodyguard and had been sent by Prince Indrajeet Thakore to keep a watch on the goings on at Rani Hyma Devi's farms.

Dr Nalini Singh made a lot of progress with Yashodhara during the next few weeks, meeting her at least twice a week, in two-hour sessions.

Yashodhara became tired after each session and Indrajeet encouraged her to go to sleep immediately after.

After the second week, Dr Nalini Singh spoke to Indrajeet and Yashodhara together to explain the next stage of the therapy.

"We have established that the main issue here is Yashodhara being molested by her stepfather. Now, with hypnotherapy, I promise to help her get back to normal as soon as possible. I hope neither of you is worried about hypnosis." Nalini Singh looked at each of them in turn. When they shook their heads, she continued, "While under hypnosis, it might seem as if the client is sleeping, but that's not exactly the case. Yashodhara will be in a semi-conscious state and will be fully aware of what's happening to her. She will be able to remember what happens during the entire time span of her hypnotic phase. In fact, she will be more responsive towards everything around her then she usually is. Are we clear so far?"

"Yes, doctor." Yashodhara answered confidently. She had developed faith in the psychiatrist and was ready to move on to the next level of treatment.

Indrajeet looked on, glad to see his wife much happier than before.

Nalini Singh explained further, "Now let me tell you how the healing happens. Whenever there's a trauma, there's a fight, flight or freeze reaction. Let's say when a thief tries to prise your jewellery in the middle of the street, you will either fight or runaway at such speed which you would have never been able to do under normal circumstances. That's because, in such situations, your gland secretes adrenaline which is what gives you the rush of power to react the way you do—way stronger than you normally can. Sometimes, there's also a third reaction, when you freeze, unable to take action. And that causes the maximum frustration, also becoming a trauma within you."

This time Yashodhara didn't wait for the doctor's look of enquiry as she nodded her head vigorously, understanding and agreeing with her.

"Now, what happens when a deer is being chased by a lion? It's very similar to a human being trapped by a thief. The deer runs faster than ever and manages to escape. After the event is over, the deer puts aside its experience and gets on with its life. But in the case of humans, the mind functions differently. It doesn't let go of the fear which created the adrenaline rush. Our minds keep anticipating similar situations to be created in the future too. And this is what creates the trauma stopping you from leading a normal life."

"Now let me explain how hypnotherapy helps. In your hypnotic state, I will take you back through your life, little by little, leading you with questions regarding key incidents. The question and answer session will be recorded for future reference. We keep doing this until we reach the point of your life when the actual incident took place. This incident is what has left a huge imprint on your mind. Now, we have to break its hold on you by building on your imagination. From what I heard from you, you froze that night and were unable to act." The doctor continued when Yashodhara nodded in agreement. "So, what we will do is use your imagination to take a strong action which will stop the other person from overpowering you. When we do that, your unconscious will deregister the incident as a trauma because you stop being a victim in your mind. This is as much as I can explain the theory of hypnotherapy to you. You will be able to understand better when it is done practically."

"It sounds miraculous, Dr Nalini. Is that how it really works?" Indrajeet asked, looking amazed. He had been listening keenly and if he had understood it correctly, Yashodhara would be cured of her mental anguish fairly easily.

The doctor smiled. "It really does work like that. The mind can be healed with powerful suggestions under the hypnotic state. Usually, all deep-rooted thoughts, both happy and sad, are buried within the unconscious. In our day-to-day lives, it is the conscious mind which is at work. The unconscious can only be healed in the hypnotic or meditative state. While meditation needs prolonged work, hypnosis happens speedily. Meditation is preferred for prevention of disease as it strengthens the immune system. Hypnosis can be used for healing a diseased mind and body."

Indrajeet nodded slowly, not uttering another word as he had turned speechless on hearing what the doctor had to say.

The trip to Mumbai went a long way in bringing Indrajeet and Yashodhara closer as they got to spend quality time with each other without the other members of the family. They went for long walks in the mornings and sometimes even went cycling, both missing their horse-riding sessions back home.

There were many restaurants serving different cuisines located within easy reach. But they bought a lot of provisions and also stocked up the fridge with veggies, fruits, meat and eggs since both of them enjoyed cooking.

Indrajeet opened his eyes when he felt a soft touch on his shoulder. "Good morning sweetheart!" He smiled on seeing his wife standing close to his side of the bed.

"Good morning! I got us coffee. Do you want to get up or shall I give it to you right here?"

"I want a kiss first." He tilted his chin, showing her his right cheek.

Yashodhara bent forward to press her mouth to his rough cheek, her lips tingling as they scraped against the morning bristle, making her smile.

Before she could move away, he pulled her on his lap, his mouth against her soft cheek. "Yash…" He drew a damp tongue over the earlobe close to him, blowing on it immediately after, making her shiver.

"Jeet…" She tilted her head back, her arms around his neck, looking up at him, not quite aware of what she wanted. She did realise though she wanted something more from him. "Please…"

Looking at the budding desire in her eyes, Indrajeet pressed his lips to the corner of her mouth. "What is it, my love?" He drew a gentle tongue over the seam of her lips.

Yashodhara trembled in his arms, her heart hammering wildly against her chest, her lips opening in a gasp only to be shell shocked when she felt his rough tongue sliding into her mouth. While her instinct was to panic, she shut her eyes to let herself savour the sensation of her husband leisurely exploring her mouth. Waves of heat rolled over her as every single nerve in her mouth came alive, his meticulous tongue slowly but surely driving her crazy.

Where were the strange mewling noises coming from? Yashodhara drew back in shock when she realised they were coming from her own throat. She opened slumberous eyes to look up at her husband and returned his wide smile with a shy one of her own.

He lifted a hand from around her waist and traced her pouting lips that had gone red with his attention. "So? That wasn't too bad, eh?" A dark eyebrow rose up to touch the thick lock of hair falling on his wide forehead.

Unaware of what she was doing, Yashodhara lifted a hand to push back the unruly lock, her fingers running through his silky hair. She shook her head, speaking in a whisper. "Bad isn't the right word for it. It was simply amazing."

"Yash…" Indrajeet buried his face against her neck, his body shuddering with desire, thrilled at the same time that they had crossed one more barrier. He moved away, much to his wife's disappointment, and said, "You pour the coffee. I'll join you in a minute." He let go of her to walk towards the adjoining bathroom, whistling on his way.

They made breakfast together in the kitchenette, Indrajeet chopping onions and tomatoes while Yashodhara beat the eggs, before folding in the grated cheese. While she fried the onions and tomatoes in a saucepan, he toasted half a dozen slices of bread in the electric toaster. Soon, she flipped the two perfectly turned out *masala omelettes* on to the plates before carrying them over to the dining table on one side of the living room. They ate their breakfast leisurely, watching the news on TV.

"Want to catch a movie?" Indrajeet asked Yashodhara as he cleared the table.

"Would love to," She nodded, "Which one?"

"There's Vidya Balan's *Tumhari Sulu*, which is a comedy drama. Or we can watch the thriller called *Ittefaq* starring Sonakshi Sinha and Sidharth Malhotra. You get to choose."

"Hmm. Let's watch both, one today and one tomorrow. What say?"

"Quite a movie buff, aren't you?" He laughed. "Great, let me book the tickets on Bookmyshow. What time are you seeing the doctor today?"

"Not today. I have an appointment for tomorrow."

"Okay, then let's catch the 11 'o clock show at PVR Icon in Oberoi Mall." He went ahead and booked the tickets for *Tumhari Sulu* and immediately called for a cab.

"Close your eyes and relax. You will go into a deep sleep as I begin to count backwards... 10, 9, 8... 7, 6, 5... 4, 3, 2, 1. Your forehead is relaxed, now your neck, your shoulders, your chest. Breathe slowly, in and out, in and out. Now relax your arms, your elbows and your hands. Continue to breathe slowly and steadily, in and out, in and out. Feel your chest relax, now your stomach, your hips, your thighs. Your knees and calves are completely at ease, as are your feet. Breathe in and out, in and out."

Dr Nalini Singh spoke to Yashodhara who was lying down on the couch, her words coming out in an unhurried fashion. When she began, her voice was at a normal pitch while she slowly reduced the sound, decibel by decibel, until Yashodhara was completely relaxed, her conscious mind silenced.

"Princess Yashodhara, it's two months after your twenty-second birthday and you are back from Sussex, living in the Jadeja palace. What are you having for breakfast?"

Yashodhara smiled, her eyes still shut, obviously recalling a happy memory, and replied, "Mama had told Shandilya, our cook, to make *paneer paratha*, my favourite. I really missed fresh *paneer parathas* when I was in England. Shandilya has truly excelled himself today. It's the best breakfast I've had in a long time."

"What did you do after that?"

"Mama has planned a surprise for me. She told me to get ready and we left by car to visit a horse farm." Yashodhara's voice grew excited. "The mare has given birth to a foal. Oh, it's so beautiful, the coat a shining black and with a white star on his forehead. Mama says she has bought him for me. Aren't I so lucky?! I have decided to call him Ebony. I think it's a fitting name for the baby. I can't wait to bring him home. But we have to wait for a few weeks."

"It's your twentieth birthday. What are you doing this morning?"

Yashodhara's lips drooped. "I got a call from Mama last evening saying she wouldn't be able to make it to England for my birthday. There was some kind of a problem with the farmers that she needed to take care of. I'm all alone."

"What about your friends? Can't you celebrate with them?"

"I have no friends, not since I left India. Before that, Chitrangada was my best friend. But it has been many years since I spoke to her. We lost touch after I moved to England."

"What about your college mates in England? You must be close to at least one or two of them."

Yashodhara shook her head, her eyes closed. "No, I chose not to have friends. The issue is they are always figuring out ways to date new guys. They expect me to be in some kind of a relationship if we are to be friends. And I don't like men."

"Why don't you like men?"

"Simply because men have the power to hurt women." Yashodhara's voice was firm with conviction. "I don't want to have anything to do with them."

"What about your male classmates then? Do you interact with them?"

"I avoid them as much as I can."

"What if any of the guys comes over and talks to you?"

"I... I make it a point never to meet their eyes. Then, they don't try to converse with me a second time."

"Alright, I understand. Now, let me take you back a few years, back to the time before you left Udaipur to go live in England. Rani Hyma Devi decided to shift you to England. What do you have to say about that?"

Yashodhara's face was contorted with anguish, as she reiterated the words she had said all those years ago, her voice laced with temper, "Mama, all my friends are here. I don't wanna go. Please don't make me give up my beautiful home and my lovely school."

"What do you think made your mother take this decision?"

Yashodhara's voice was dry and hoarse when she replied, "My stepfather raped me a month back. He beat me black and blue and my mother didn't want anyone to know about what had happened. She kept me back in my room, taking care of me all by herself. She didn't want anyone in our kingdom to know what had happened to me as she didn't want to bring shame on me. That's also why she didn't want me to meet or talk to my friends." The anxiety in her voice heightened as she continued in a choked whisper, "Not even my best friend Chitrangada. Mama didn't want anyone to know what had happened to me," she repeated, "She wanted to save me from being shamed by the society." Her eyeballs moved rapidly behind her shut eyelids even as her body trembled.

"Why would society shame you?"

"Because I was raped." Yashodhara was shouting now.

"But that's not your fault. It's..."

"Of course, it's my fault. Why else would my stepfather rape me?" Tears were pouring down her cheeks and running into her hair by now as Yashodhara voiced her guilt.

"It could be because your stepfather was a bad man and he wanted to force himself on you. You were but a child."

Yashodhara shook her head. "Whatever the reason, I am the one living with the shame. People will laugh at me if they know about it. That's why Mama didn't want me to speak about it. She says that even the walls have ears and insists that I should not speak about it even to her, my own mother." Her voice broke with remembered grief.

"Let's go back a month, to the fateful evening. How did it all start?"

Yashodhara's voice was a hushed whisper of horror as she recalled her misery of so long ago. "Mama went out for the evening and I was in my room, doing my home-work. My stepfather suddenly walked in and said that he wanted to talk to me, have a father-daughter conversation that had been long overdue. I… I know he is a good husband to my mother since more than a year. But, somehow, I couldn't ever like him. I… er… don't like the way he looks at me."

"How does he look at you?"

"He always stares at my breasts. I try my best to sit low in my chair at the dining table—those are the times we come face-to-face every day, during meals—but even then, he keeps on ogling."

"Didn't your mother know what he was doing? I mean, didn't she notice him watching you?"

"He's sneaky. He only watches me when she isn't looking."

"Why don't you tell your mother what he does?"

Yashodhara shook her head slowly from side to side. "I don't want to tell her."

"Is there a reason for that?"

"My mother had been very sad before she met my stepfather. I think she missed my father. But she became happier after meeting my stepfather and marrying him. I don't want to make her unhappy by complaining to her about him." There was no hesitation in Yashodhara's voice when she uttered those words.

"So, what happened when he came to your room that evening?"

"He went and sat on my bed and invited me to go sit with him." There was a grimace of revulsion on Yashodhara's face.

"Did you do that?"

"Of course not. He told me to call him 'Papa' and I refused. Then I tried to escape from the room, but the top bolt on the door was firmly in place. Before I could reach up to pull it down—I wasn't tall enough and had to jump high—he caught me. He pulled me by my hair and squeezed my breasts… it was damn painful. Then, he lifted me, carrying me to the bed before dumping me on it."

"Didn't you fight?"

"I kept kicking him until he suddenly yelled with pain. That was when he dumped me on the bed, I think. Finding myself free suddenly, I rolled over the bed, dropped down from the other side and ran into the bathroom, before locking myself in." Yashodhara sounded breathless as if she was running just now.

"And then?"

"For a few seconds, I thought I was safe. But he pounded on the door so hard that the hinges broke. He saw me cowering on one side and came towards me, a leer on his face…" Yashodhara was sobbing by now, a keening sound escaping her throat.

Nalini Singh paused only for a couple of seconds before saying, "Now, Princess Yashodhara, listen to me carefully. Take your eyes off your stepfather and look around the bathroom. There must be something, a broom or a cleaning brush, something that you can use as a weapon… look around carefully and tell me what you see."

Yashodhara's eyes rolled behind her eyelids as if she was looking around for something. "There's a mop, with a long wooden handle. But it's in the far corner."

"Stop cowering and get up, right now. You are smaller than him, maybe. But you are definitely swifter. Take a leap, pick up that mop and beat him up, as hard as you can."

Yashodhara's arms and legs flailed as she mentally took a leap to the other corner of the bathroom, even as the doctor continued with her instructions. "So, now that you have the mop in your hand, beat him on his back and his legs, wherever you can reach."

Yashodhara's body moved this way and that as with a deep scowl on her forehead, she mentally beat up her stepfather until she fell back on the floor, exhausted.

"See him lying on the floor in a faint. Can you see him?"

"Yes, I can." There was a maniacal grin on Yashodhara's face now.

"He can't harm you, after all, can he?"

"No, he can't." There was glee on her face even if Yashodhara's voice was weak.

"See, you are a winner now. There's no pain in your body or your mind. You are completely healed."

"Yes, I'm completely healed." There was triumph in Yashodhara's voice.

It was another fifteen minutes before the doctor slowly brought Yashodhara to the present and then woke her up from her trance state.

Yashodhara sat up, feeling extraordinarily refreshed, before getting up and going to sit on the sofa adjacent to where Nalini was seated. "What happened, doctor?"

Dr Nalini Singh smiled. "All these years, there was an imprint on your mind, that of being raped by your stepfather. The incident is long dead and gone, in the past. There's less than one chance in a million that it will happen again. But your conscious mind was soaked with fear that every man who came within ten feet of you, might harm or hurt you. Now, with imagination, I implanted the idea in your unconscious…"

"That I defended myself against Jaswantlal and beat him up with the wooden handle of the mop in my bathroom." Yashodhara gave the doctor a wide smile.

"You remember!" There was no surprise on Nalini's face. "That's precisely what I set out to do. You are completely healed now, Yasho. Your fear of men is gone."

"Is it so simple?" There was awe in Yashodhara's voice. "Can we ask Jeet to join us here?"

"Of course." Nalini rang the bell for her receptionist and asked him to call Indrajeet inside the living-consulting room. "Congratulations, Jeet," she greeted him, when he entered, "Please take a seat."

Indrajeet went and sat next to Yashodhara, taking her hand in his. He looked from one woman to the other, his eyes lingering on his wife's smiling face. She appeared so happy and carefree, like he had never seen her before.

"What's up?" he asked, turning to the doctor, pulling his gaze away from his wife's glowing face with an effort.

"This is it. We're done. Yasho is completely cured of her fear. You can go back home and lead a normal life." There was absolute satisfaction and joy in the doctor's voice, of a job well done. It had taken six weeks, but her patient was completely normal now.

The doctor explained to them how it had worked, how the imprint on her memory had been erased using her imagination to change the circumstances of her past experience. "The incident is dead and buried. There's nothing we can do about what happened earlier. But we can change the way we perceive the experience. Because Yasho triumphed over her stepfather in her imagination, when in the state of hypnosis, a new memory has been written over the old traumatic memory that has been erased. Now, she has no fear in her, not of her stepfather nor of other men."

Indrajeet shook his head in amazement. "That's so awesome, doctor." He turned to Yashodhara and asked, "How do you feel, Yash?"

She gave him a wide grin, holding his hand tightly in hers, "On top of the world. I don't remember feeling so good at any time in the recent past."

He grinned as he moved forward to press his lips to hers, forgetting for a moment that they were still in Dr Nalini Singh's consulting room. Yashodhara kissed him right back, feeling buoyant as her heartbeat soared in excitement, not an iota of fear dogging her any more. She could freely respond to her husband's physical overtures.

They broke apart after a few minutes, both remembering the doctor at the same time. They turned towards the sofa where Nalini had been seated and sighed with relief when they found it empty. Indrajeet and Yashodhara laughed at each other, silently appreciating the doctor's tactfulness.

They said 'goodbye' to the doctor and thanked her vociferously before taking an cab back to their apartment. They were in the lift when Yashodhara hugged her husband's arm with both of hers, her heart overflowing with love for him.

"Jeet." Her voice was a whisper in his ear. "Do you mind if we stay back in Mumbai for the rest of the two weeks or do you want us to return home immediately?" She looked into his face, soft colour blooming on her cheeks, her green eyes beseeching him to agree.

Indrajeet laughed. "I was going to ask you the same thing. And of course, we can. Unless you want to go somewhere more exotic for a proper honeymoon." He raised a dark eyebrow, giving her the choice while wanting to know if she was open to taking their relationship to the next level.

"I love our little apartment and I feel a special attachment to it since this is where we've been staying while I was undergoing the treatment. Now that I am completely cured, I think this is the perfect place for a honeymoon. Don't you think? And Jeet," she pressed closer to his ear, "everything will be fine, right?" Her smile dimmed.

"Everything will be perfect. You have me, right?" Indrajeet gave her a cocky grin, bringing the bright smile back to her face.

16

Munshi Kilachand called MLA Hirji as late as eleven in the night. Hirji took the call, ready to blast the other man off. Kilachand cut him off, saying, "Hirji, sir, *hungama ho gaya*. The lab results of the plants have reached the police department. And now, Bhupinder Sharma, the IG of police, has also been roped in. We are in deep shit. Please, only you can do something."

"Shut up, man. Who gave you the right to disturb me so late at night?" Hirji shouted into his phone. "It's not my problem. You are making a lot of money in this, right? You sort it out. Listen; if my name is dragged into it, I'll break your bones. Yes, that's exactly what I plan to do!" His shouting had turned into a snarl as Hirji wiped the drops of sweat dripping down his face with a hand towel.

"But sir, what can I do?" There was panic in Kilachand's voice. "If Rani Hyma Devi gets to know I have been a party to this, she'll kill me." He quaked at the thought. He had been running this illegal trading of poppy since the last four years. In the beginning, his conscience had troubled him a lot. But soon, he had convinced himself he needed the money. He wasn't rich like the Rani and unlike her he had four daughters. Well, he decided to forget that she paid him an exorbitant salary and also paid for his children's education from nursery to graduation. Who wouldn't want to make more money on the side? It was a golden opportunity and it fell into his lap when Hirji's man had approached him. It had taken Hirji just two months to convince Kilachand that with so many acres of land, the Rani wouldn't even sense something amiss if they grew illegal poppy instead of wheat or barley.

"Listen, man, she's just a woman. You are the one person she trusts and you are the one who has been managing the lands since the death of Raja Ratansinh Jadeja. And you say that the Jadejas have the license to grow the plant on ten acres, right? We will be just stretching it a little bit more. There won't be any trouble. If and when someone comes asking, I am there, right? I wield a lot of power in the government. No one can shake me."

This dialogue uttered by the MLA happened four years ago. Over the years, the ten acres' license had been stretched to accommodate one hundred and fifty acres. Each year, the number of fields growing poppies kept increasing. Every time the business was expanded to include more land, Kilachand had winced but stayed silent, since his cut in the profits had been increasing by leaps and bounds. His confidence had grown since he really didn't have to lift a finger other than hedging the account books. Between Hirji and Kilachand, they had also managed to employ a few *gundas* from the neighbouring states to keep the operation running smoothly.

They had been lucky Amarchand Khatri, a fifth-generation farmer, had been equally greedy. Built like a truck, and with a menacing demeanour, Khatri had brought some of the farmers under his control. The illegal poppy was grown in the fields of at least a dozen farmers.

What they hadn't expected was the Rani getting her only daughter married to the Thakore scion. They hadn't sensed trouble even when the marriage took place. It was a few weeks later, when Indrajeet brought the plants back to the accounts office and faced Kilachand with them, he realised that there might be major trouble coming their way.

"*Munshiji*, I brought these plants from the far away fields. Let me see," Indrajeet opened his phone to check some pictures, "these are from the field marked no. 87. At a glance, I can see these are poppy plants. I want you to send them to the government lab for testing, so that we have legal proof. What I understood from the *Rani Saheba* is that we have license to grow poppies only on the field marked no. 62 which is ten acres. If that's the case, then we are growing illegal poppy on Jadeja farms. Do you know who's in charge of field no. 87 and further?" Indrajeet had pinned the *munshi* with his sharp gaze.

Kilachand had shrugged, shivering inside as he looked into the prince's stern, unwavering gaze. "I'll need to check, *Kunwarji*. I can tell you the day after tomorrow."

"Why do you need that long? You must be having a list of the field owners, right?"

"*Ji, ji*. Of course, I have. But, you know, I am growing old and I don't have anyone to help me here. I..." He stopped when he realised the pit he was digging himself into.

"If that's the case, I'll send my man over today afternoon itself. He'll also get a computer set up here in the office and make sure all relevant information is fed into it. Then it will be much easier to manage the fields." Indrajeet offered the *munshi* an instantaneous solution.

Kilachand understood that matters were fast sliding out of his control, and there wasn't much he could do about it. He resorted to emotional blackmail which had always worked with the royals. "*Theek hai, Kunwarji*, if that's what you want. I realise now an old man's service doesn't count for much nowadays. I've been handling everything even when the Raja was alive, but I can see times have changed." He sniffed loudly.

Indrajeet smiled. "Okay, *munshiji*, have it your way. Keep the list of farmers ready for me the day after tomorrow. I'll come to collect it by eleven in the morning. Will that be convenient for you?"

Munshi's sniff was louder this time, his confidence growing as he had got his own way with the prince. "I will try my best."

"Do that. Let me do something in the meanwhile. I'll get the plants to the laboratory myself, since you are going to be busy." With that, Prince Indrajeet Thakore snatched the plants from right under Kilachand's nose and carried them away. The *munshi* turned pale as he had had other plans for those plants. He had intended to burn them. He would have got away with it too, using the old age card and loyalty factor once again. Now the opportunity was lost forever.

He had got the list ready, inserting fake names in the place of the real names of the farmers and had it ready for the prince at the appointed hour. Only, the prince hadn't come personally, but sent a servant to collect the list.

And today, almost six weeks later, the laboratory had sent a report to the Jadeja farm office, along with a show cause notice.

It was all fine for the MLA to accuse Kilachand of making a lot of money from the illegal project. But it was Hirji himself who got the biggest chunk of the pie. These politicians! Bah! They were like rats slinking off the sinking ship. Now it was up to Kilachand to deal with the problem. It was a good thing that both the prince and princess were not in town. With that positive thought in mind, the *munshi* took a walk, hoping to clear his mind as he needed to urgently come up with a disaster management plan.

In the end, Jaswantlal Diwekar was released from prison, three months before his term got over. He received his old clothes which had been left with the jail warden, putting them on with shaking hands. He was going to be free, at last, after being incarcerated for thirteen years and nine months. His clothes hung on his shrunken frame, about seventy-five per cent of his hair having turned white. He had had his beard trimmed and shaped today. *Not bad,* he thought, staring into the small and spotted hand mirror.

Time to go meet his ex-wife!

Bhupinder Sharma's assistant made a routine weekly call to the jail to enquire about Jaswantlal Sharma. Nitara went back to the IG's office and said, "Sir, the prisoner you asked me to find out about, Jaswantlal Diwekar…"

"What about him?" Bhupinder looked up from his laptop to ask his assistant. He had just received an email from Prince Indrajeet Thakore, copied to Rani Hyma Devi, regarding illegal plantation of poppies, and had forgotten all about the Rani's ex-husband. His assistant Nitara's job was to call the jail every week to ensure that the prisoner was still serving his sentence.

"He was released two hours ago."

"What?!" Bhupinder Sharma pushed back his chair to stand up with a jerk. "Are you sure?"

"Yes sir. I spoke to the jail warden to confirm the news."

"Shit! Get the driver to bring my car out NOW. I need to rush." He had taken his cell out and was calling

Rani Hyma Devi on speed dial. Nitara ran out to follow his instructions, understanding the emergency from her boss's tone of voice.

17

"I'll make coffee." Indrajeet walked away from Yashodhara the moment they entered their apartment. His instinct was to jump on her and make love to her, all at once. But no. It wouldn't do. He had waited for so many months. What would a few more hours matter? His hands trembled as he took the milk carton from the fridge and poured some into a pan for heating. It was only then he remembered that he had forgotten to switch on the electric coffee percolator. He took deep breaths to control his libido. His wife was fully recovered. The doctor had made it amply clear. It was also obvious from the way Yashodhara smiled at him and even touched him voluntarily, way more than she had done so far. But he had to give her, her space. He wasn't an animal, damnit!

Yashodhara stared at her husband's broad back as he stood at the stove in the kitchenette. She had been sure that he would want to make love to her the moment they stepped inside their temporary home. Hadn't she even made it clear in words? But what was he doing, making coffee neither of them wanted or needed? Her body, that had been mostly asleep, had been in a slow state of awakening since the night she had begun to sleep in his arms. Now, with her fear completely gone, her needs had come to the fore and she so looked forward to Indrajeet making love to her. But what was wrong with the man? Why was he so far away from her?

Didn't he want her anymore? Yashodhara pushed the thought away the moment it rose within her. Not possible. She knew for a fact that her husband loved her and wanted her. A slow smile stretched across her lips. Knowing him for the sensitive man he was, Indrajeet was probably keeping away from her, under the mistaken impression that she might want her space. That must be it!

The moment the thought crossed her mind, Yashodhara got up from the sofa and walked silently on bare feet and hugged her husband from behind, her breasts tingling on contact with his hard, strongly muscled back, as she turned off the gas stove with one hand. "Don't you want me, Jeet?"

Indrajeet groaned as he turned around in her arms, just remembering to switch off the percolator. "Too much, Yash." He crushed her in his arms, his lips at her ear. "So much that I'm worried of scaring you off." He nibbled her earlobe gently, curbing the instinct to take a bite, his tongue tracing the shape of her ear.

"Never that! You, my Jeet, can never scare me off. Please love me, Jeet. My body is clamouring for you." Yashodhara turned her head to nip his earlobe, thrilled to hear him groan again. Suddenly, she felt the floor shift as he lifted her in his arms to carry her towards the bedroom. She threw her arms around his neck, giggling. "I must say you are a strong man, able to lift my bulk."

Indrajeet looked at her intently as he placed her on the bed, none too gently, his hands feverishly pulling at his shirt buttons. "I adore your body and think it's just perfect."

"Let me." A blushing Yashodhara was on her knees on the bed as she reached out to her husband, pulling eagerly at each button before peeling his shirt off his wide shoulders, her eyes clinging to his naked torso. "Jeet..." She gulped, her eyes going wide as she stared at all that shining bronze skin which was peppered with dark whorls of springy hair. She raised a hand to stroke his chest, a soft laugh tumbling out from her mouth as she looked up into his burning velvety gaze, her own hazel green eyes slumberous with desire. She took her hand off his chest to unpin the silver brooch holding her sari in place before pulling it off her shoulder, revelling in his heated brown gaze roving over her chest, her nipples pushing against the restrictions of her bra and blouse.

"Let me." Indrajeet moved her hands away to slip the tiny hooks out of their fastenings at the front of her blouse, his breath coming in gasps as her cleavage came into view. "Yash, you look gorgeous," he said, pushing the front flaps of her blouse away from her luscious breasts, eyeing the creamy lace covering her bounty. He swore when her blouse refused to budge as the two flaps were also caught up by the buttons at the shoulders, making Yashodhara laugh again.

"Allow me." She swiftly removed her blouse before unhooking her bra at the back, a soft gasp escaping her throat when Indrajeet pulled the bra at the front and threw it on the floor. Her eyelids felt heavy as she watched his throat work when he cupped the underside of her breasts. "Jeet… love me, please."

"With pleasure, my sweetheart." Indrajeet bent down to stroke the tip of her right breast with a rough tongue, making her moan with the pleasure exploding in her body, creating a wet pool between her legs. Yashodhara had never felt such pleasure, not having associated anything but pain where her breasts were concerned. But her husband drove her mad as he pleasured her with his warm mouth and tongue, before gently biting the engorged flesh above the tip, making her jump off the bed and into his arms. "Like it?" He asked, lifting his gaze to hers, his mouth still against her breast.

"Love it, Jeet. I want more."

"I'll give you more." He took the nipple into his mouth and sucked on it, making her mewl in rapture. She held his head between her hands, pulling him closer to her body. She couldn't get enough of Indrajeet's lovemaking as he pleasured her breasts, his hands and mouth arousing her to a fever pitch, until Yashodhara thrashed her legs restlessly. Without taking his mouth off her breast, he managed to pull her sari out of the petticoat and threw it over his shoulder. His hands were shaking as he tried in vain to pull the knot off the petticoat. "Help me, Yash and get this damned thing off," he growled, moving his mouth to the other tip.

"Eh?!" Yashodhara opened her eyes to look down at his dark head against her pale flesh and sighed in delight. "What?"

He looked up at his wife, grinning at the dark colour flaring on her cheeks. "Can you help me take off your petticoat? I'm unable to open the knot."

"Mmm… okay." Yashodhara pressed her lips to the top of his head, still unclear as to what he wanted her to do, as she was lost in the new sensations hitting her upper body, setting off a chain reaction in her womb.

Indrajeet shook his head, a grin on his face as he realised that his wife was in no state to understand his instructions. He lifted his head from her chest and was rewarded with her cries of protests. His grin turned wider as he looked at her. "In a minute, sweetheart. I…"

"Come to me." Yashodhara lifted her arms wide, completely unconscious of her jiggling breasts, actually revelling in her husband's avid gaze on them.

"In a minute, Yash. Once I have this petticoat off you," he growled, taking her hand and placing it against the complicated knot. "Will you remove this damn thing?" He gave her a mock glare.

"Oh! So, Prince Indrajeet Thakore, who's an expert in boxing and swashbuckling, can't manage to open a simple knot?" Yashodhara teased him, her green eyes glowing with mischief as she swiftly unknotted her petticoat and shimmied out of it.

His coffee brown eyes promised retribution even as they shifted to her bouncing breasts as she did a little dance while she pushed the petticoat down her legs. His laughter caught in his throat as her long and voluptuous legs were laid bare to his gaze. "Yash… I love your body." He lifted both hands to stroke them down the shape of her thighs, bending his head to press his lips to the tiny cream lace panties hiding her femininity from his view.

"Jeet…" Yashodhara fell back on the bed, shutting her eyes as she revelled in his lovemaking. She gasped when she felt his hands at the sides of her hips before he pulled her panties down, inch by treacherous inch, until they slid off her feet. "Jeet… what are you doing?" She jumped off the bed when she felt his mouth at the apex of her thighs.

"Pleasuring both of us," he said, before stroking his tongue into the folds of her feminine core.

Yashodhara was lost by now, in a sea of hedonistic pleasure as his hands caressed her breasts while his lips and tongue made love to the most private part of her body. It wasn't long before an orgasm ripped her apart, making her moan long and hard, her hands clutching her husband's shoulders in a fierce grip. She felt as if her body might spiral off into space.

Indrajeet climbed up to lie next to his wife, holding her close against his chest, rocking her body gently. "Are you okay?" He asked her softly, his eyes roving over her flushed features.

Yashodhara opened her heavy eyelids with an effort, looking into his eyes, even as a slow smile lit up her face. Tracing a hand over his manly cheek, she said, "I've never been better, Jeet. I love you."

Indrajeet turned his face to catch her thumb into his mouth and sucked on it, his teeth nipping the pad. "I love you too, sweetheart."

"But, Jeet, what about you?" She touched her hand to the belt holding up his pants. "You haven't even undressed fully."

He looked into her face, his brown eyes glowing with banked desire. "In time, my love. I just wanted to be sure that you don't feel your space invaded."

"Jeet..." A shimmer of tears glistened in Yashodhara's eyes as she stared at the man, her husband, whom she had fallen in love with. He was an amazing human being. Wasn't she lucky! She got out of his arms to unbuckle his belt, before removing the button that held his pants in place. Pulling the zip down, she slid the pants off his long, muscular legs before taking them off completely.

Indrajeet lay back on the bed, his hands under his head, a look of amusement on his face as he caught the determined expression on his lovely wife's face. He wondered how far she would go. He choked the very next second, the levity wiped off his face as he felt Yashodhara bury her face against his taut manhood that was still trapped in his briefs, realising that she was simply mimicking his actions of before.

He was even more amazed when she hooked her thumbs into the sides of his briefs and pulled them down swiftly to throw them on the floor.

Her eyes went wide when she eyed his shaft that sprung forth from a bed of thick hair. Fascinated, she rubbed her hand over him, before taking his manhood in both her hands. "Jeet…" She looked up at him, not really knowing what to do next, meeting the look of delight and mischief in his sensuous, volatile eyes. "I don't know… I… do you like me touching you?" she asked him in a hesitant voice, her hands inadvertently caressing him, while she wasn't really aware of the effect she was having on him.

Indrajeet placed his hand over hers as she stroked his length. "Does my tightening shaft tell you something?"

"You've been growing bigger and harder as I'm touching you. What does that mean?"

"That I love your hands on me," he groaned as she gripped him firmly with both her hands. "Yash, I need to get inside you. Will you let me?"

Her hands stopped as she looked up at him from her position on her knees between his legs. "What's stopping you, Jeet? I'm absolutely fine. I…" she stroked his length with both her hands, revelling in the feel of steel encased in velvet, "I feel no fear at all. Actually, I can't wait to have you inside me."

"Yash…" With a groan, Indrajeet got up to push her down on the bed before mounting her, placing the tip of his manhood against the entrance to her femininity. Encouraged by her hands on his hips, he entered her slowly, with a grunt, moving bit by bit, his teeth clenched as he allowed her body to get used to him. Once he was deeply sheathed inside her, he buried his face against her neck, growling, "Are you fine?"

"I… am okay. But I want something more." There was confusion in Yashodhara's voice as she tried to shift her legs under the weight of his. He felt amazing, deeply fitted inside her. But her body begged for something that seemed out of reach.

"I'm sure," gasped Indrajeet, torn between laughter and the groan that emanated from the depth of his chest as he lifted himself on his elbows pressed on the bed on both sides of her, pulling himself out of her before thrusting into her immediately after. Soon, he was riding her hard, encouraged by the moans coming from her throat, losing control as he rode even harder as his body begged for release. He gritted his teeth and held on for dear life until he felt her gush around him before spilling his seed within her womb, groaning long and hard as he climaxed like he had never had before. His body limp, Indrajeet fell on Yashodhara before moving to the side with an effort, and pulled her close to his chest.

Soon, the two of them fell into a deep slumber, cuddled close to each other, totally unaware of the hell breaking loose back home.

Indrajeet came wide awake when he heard the soft ring of his cell phone. What? Where was his phone? He forgot the ringing phone when he moved his body and felt Yashodhara's silky skin against his. He smiled, bending down to place a swift kiss on her shoulder before turning in the direction of the sound. His eyes finally fell on his pants lying where Yashodhara had thrown them, a few feet away from the bed. He gently pushed his wife's sleeping body away from his and got up, walked swiftly and lifted his pants off the floor. And just then the phone stopped ringing. He put his hand in the right-hand side pocket and pulled out the phone to see who it was. There were four missed calls—one from a strange number, one from Rani Hyma Devi and two from his father. What the hell! He looked at the time. It was barely seven in the evening. Was there some kind of an emergency?

He pushed the button to speed dial his father's number to have Gajendar pick it up on the second ring. "Jeet, can you please get back home ASAP? There's trouble brewing with the farmers for one thing." His father didn't sugar coat the situation.

"And Yashodhara's stepfather is out of jail for another. Talking of which, how is Yasho? Is she better than before?"

"Papa." Indrajeet rubbed his eyes to dispel the sleepiness, automatically turning to look at his wife who was sprawled naked on the king-size bed, a smile stretching his lips. "Yash's fine. She's completely recovered. You please don't worry about anything, Papa. We'll be there tonight. Is Meghnath still in charge at the Jadeja farms?"

"He is, Jeet. That's how I got to know there's trouble. So far, it's only a whisper. Though it could blow out of control, he says."

Indrajeet digested the information. Meghnath wasn't one to panic. If he said that it could blow out of control, then the situation must be bad. "Okay, Papa. I'll talk to him. And what's with Rani Hyma Devi's ex-husband? Do you expect him to create trouble?" He turned around again when he noticed Yashodhara stirring on the bed, his shaft springing to attention immediately, bringing a smile to his lips.

"I don't really know. Bhupinder Sharma, the IG of police called to ask me for your mobile number. Did he call you?"

"I think he did since there's a missed call from a new number. Okay, Papa. I'll quickly call the other two numbers and also Meghnath to find out what's happening. You take care and don't worry. I'll…"

"And Jeet, before you go, I almost forgot. You have an unexpected guest from the US. Juliana Davies says that she went to college with you. She arrived in the afternoon and we have put her up in the guest suite in the west wing."

"Shit! What is she doing there?"

"You don't want her here?"

"Papa, she loves to create trouble. I…" He stopped when he felt two soft arms closing around his waist as a feminine hand moved south to stroke his arousal. "It's okay, Papa. I'll talk to you when we get there."

"We are getting where?" Yashodhara rubbed her breasts against his smooth back, her pelvis pressed to his taut buttocks, her right hand holding his shaft as she brushed a thumb over the tip.

"Yash…" Indrajeet groaned as the phone fell out of his hands, making no noise as it hit the deep pile carpet. He turned to gather her in his arms, his lips closing over hers as he kissed her thirstily. It was a while before he lifted his head to look at her pouting red lips, trying to recall his father's words. "Yash, we need to rush back home. Something has come up. I…" He choked mid-sentence when she went down on her knees and took him in her mouth, her tongue stroking the head, even as she gently nibbled him. "Sweetheart, listen, we don't have…"

The phone rang loudly this time, as it was out of his pants' pocket.

Yashodhara moved her head away to say, "Ignore it, Jeet." The princess gave the order imperiously, and realised just in time that she was addressing her husband, who was also a prince in his own right and added, "Please".

Indrajeet couldn't help smiling as he bent down to take his phone. "I can't, sweetheart. There are too many things happening back home. It's your mother on the phone." His smile turned into a grin when he saw his wife grimace before speaking into the phone. "Hello Aunty. I was just going to call you. Is anything the matter?"

"Hello, Mr Thakore, this is Bhupinder Sharma…"

"The Inspector General of Police. I've heard a lot about you, sir. Is the Rani's ex-husband creating too much trouble?"

The IG laughed. "You heard the news. Well, actually, the man has arrived at the Jadeja palace. He insists he's repentant about what he did all those years ago. Believe me, I still don't quite know what he actually did. It's just that he insists on meeting Princess Yashodhara and is refusing to go away before he does that. I would happily kick his ass, it's just that Rani Hyma Devi has gone ballistic. She doesn't want him to go free nor does she want him to remain at the palace. I just wanted to check if the princess is with you."

Indrajeet frowned, trying to understand the situation, his mind not functioning fully with his wife's naked form draped all over him. When she realised he was more interested in his phone calls, Yashodhara had got up to press her body close to his, hoping to distract him, her lips tracing the contours of his chest. "Yes sir, Yashodhara is with me. We are not in town, but will be getting back tonight." He pressed a hand to the back of Yashodhara's shaking head, to push her face into his chest and almost yelped when he felt her bite his flat male nipple. "I trust you can deal with the man until I get back home, Mr Sharma?"

"But, of course, Thakore *saheb*. No worries there." The IG cut the phone call.

"Yash!" Indrajeet caught her thick hair in his hand and pulled her face away from his chest. "Listen, sweetheart, we…"

"I don't want to go home. I want to make love with you, now." She pouted at her husband, the light in her hazel green eyes calling out to him. "Didn't you say that we could stay on for two more weeks?" She turned away from him in mock anger, confident her husband would reach out to pacify her.

Unable to resist, Indrajeet hugged her from behind, bringing her lush bottom against his clamouring manhood, his hands rising up to cup her breasts. "Listen, my love, there's not one, but three emergencies awaiting us back home. We need to pack and leave immediately." He tweaked the tips of her breasts between his thumbs and forefingers, his lips seeking the pulse at her neck.

Yashodhara tilted her head back on his shoulder, a mischievous look in her eyes. "Kiss me!" she commanded her husband.

Indrajeet obliged her, unable to resist as his mouth clung to hers in a deep kiss, his tongue mating with hers. He seemed capable of forgetting his own name just now.

When he lifted his face to look down at her, his wife smiled up at him. "Tell you what. Why don't you charter a plane and we'll make love quickly? All we need to do is get dressed and go. We'll get back to our honeymoon here once the emergencies are dealt with. What say?"

"I say yes, yes and yes," said her husband, crushing her lips with another kiss.

"Don't forget to charter our flight," said his wife sweetly, bending down to pick his phone.

"Sure, Your Highness," responded Indrajeet with a grin, taking joy in giving her rounded bottom a playful slap, before taking the phone from her.

"You'll need to kiss my butt better if you want to get anywhere near me." Yashodhara challenged him.

He wiggled his brows at her, not replying to her comment as the phone was picked up at the other end. The flight was all set to leave at 8.30. "*Chalo*, we have twenty minutes to leave."

"That's plenty of time to apologise to my bum and to make love to me." She giggled when her husband jumped on her as she lay on the bed, obliging her every whim.

Indrajeet called Meghnath on the way to the airport. "What's up, Meghnath?"

"There's word going around that they are planning to set fire to all the illegal poppy fields in the middle of the night. It's just that if the wind chances to blow in the wrong direction, many of the farm houses will perish." Meghnath explained the situation briefly.

"How much time do we have?"

"They have planned it for one in the morning. That should give us…"

"…five hours. Do you know Bhajrang Varma?"

"The old man who's an inspiration to all the farmers? I know where he lives."

"Go to him. Tell him that I sent you at *Rajmata* Santhini Devi's behest. Explain the situation to him, exactly as it is. He'll guide you. I should land in Udaipur by ten or so. I'll be in touch."

"*Ji, Kunwarji.*"

"What's happening?" They got out of the OLA to walk to the Chhatrapati Shivaji Airport terminal. Checking in took no time at all as they were led to a private gate where their plane was waiting, its engine running.

They entered the air craft and got settled in their comfortable seats before Indrajeet replied. "One is that the Jadeja farmers are planning to set fire to a hundred and forty acres of poppy fields as the poppy is being grown illegally. The second is that your stepfather is out of jail and is in your home…" When Yashodhara gasped, he took her hand in his, before continuing, "the IG of police, Bhupinder Sharma is also there, keeping an eye on him. It's just that Jaswantlal Diwekar insists on meeting you." He looked at his wife, a look of mild worry on his face. If it had been possible, he would rather have not told her about this. But she had to know, his brave princess. It was up to her how she dealt with the situation. She wouldn't thank him for taking the decision on her behalf.

"I'll meet him." Yashodhara squared her shoulders, her hand tightening around her husband's. "I'm not scared of him. I might even kick his ass."

Indrajeet reached out to press his mouth to her soft lips. "I'm proud of you, my sweetheart."

She pressed her head to his shoulder, asking, "And what's the third emergency?"

Indrajeet grimaced. "My ex-girlfriend has landed up at our home and has taken residence."

"Were… are you in love with her?" She looked deeply into his eyes.

"No." Indrajeet shook his head. "There was a time when I considered marrying her. But I was never in love with her."

Yashodhara nodded. "How could you be? You were always meant to love me," she declared, reaching out to kiss him. "It looks like I have more than one ass to kick."

Indrajeet laughed. "It seems so. I wish there wasn't an air hostess hovering around. I want to bury myself in you." He whispered in her ear.

"Let's make love with words. Let me tell you what I'd like to do with your manhood." Her hand traced the shape of his crotch as she spoke in detail. "I want to take you in my mouth…"

They were surprised when they landed at Maharana Pratap Airport at Udaipur, unaware of how time had flown.

"**L**et's go to your home first and face your stepfather before I take off for the poppy farms." Indrajeet quirked an eyebrow at his wife as they settled into the car waiting for them at the airport.

"Okay."

Indrajeet called up his father to inform him that they had landed and were on their way to Bhatewar. They reached quickly as the Jadeja palace wasn't very far from the airport. All the lights were on despite the lateness of the hour, the front door left open.

Indrajeet and Yashodhara got out of the car. Before they stepped in, he hugged her tightly. "I love you, my sweetheart."

"And I love you, Jeet." There was a serene look on her face as she looked back at him with love shining in her eyes. "You don't need to worry. In a way I am glad to get the chance to meet him. This will bring closure."

Indrajeet nodded his head. His princess was right. "Let's go."

Rani Hyma Devi looked up when they walked into the main hall. "Yasho…" She came in a half-run towards her daughter, throwing her arms around her. "I'm sorry, my child. I'm so sorry that I couldn't save you from this. I…"

"It's alright, Mama. Please don't be upset. I've come a long way since those days, Mama." She hugged her mother back before turning towards the two men sitting on adjacent sofas. "Hello Bhupinder Uncle, how have you been?"

The IG got up from his seat and walked towards Yashodhara once he was sure that Indrajeet's eyes were fixed on their unwanted guest. "I'm fine, Princess. And how have you been? Marriage suits you; I see."

Yashodhara grinned at the policeman. "Indrajeet suits me, Uncle."

Rani Hyma Devi turned to look at her daughter, noticing her blooming cheeks for the first time, before looking at her son-in-law, a look of wonder on her face as she realised the truth in her daughter's words.

Bhupinder laughed at the princess's answer. "I can see that, my child. Come, there's someone here who insists on meeting you."

"Yes, I heard about that." Yashodhara walked forward to face the man who had turned her life upside down over the last so many years. Jaswantlal Diwekar was nothing like she remembered. The last time she saw him, she had been small, four inches short of five feet. He had seemed like a giant, his tall and broad frame threatening. Today, she was the height of five feet, ten inches, and built like an Amazon. The shrunken old man, cowering on the sofa, tears threatening to fall from his cataract-ridden eyes, appeared like no threat to her, not at all. The newly healed Yashodhara wouldn't have minded taking on the giant he had been, either.

All she could feel was pity for the man as he got up from the sofa, his hunched and stooped body limping forward. "I'm sorry, Princess Yashodhara. I'm terribly sorry for the wrong I did you." He brought his hands together in apology. "I hope you have it in your large heart to forgive me." Tears poured down his withered cheeks as he begged for her forgiveness.

Rani Hyma Devi watched on, anguish on her face as she looked from her ex-husband to her daughter, tears in her own eyes.

"You don't matter, do you hear, Jaswantlal Diwekar? I don't care enough to know if you are alive or dead. But, well, maybe we could accommodate you in the home for the aged that Mama and I have built for people like you, who have no family to take care of them."

The royal princess turned away from the old man and called out to a servant. "Make sure that this man reaches Shanti Vilas immediately." Once he was escorted away, she turned to her mother and gave her a reassuring smile before addressing her along with Bhupinder Sharma. "You both will have to please excuse Jeet and me. We need to go elsewhere urgently. Jeet, shall we?" She looked at her husband, an eyebrow raised as if to ask him if she had done well.

"That was perfect," Indrajeet walked up to whisper in his wife's ear, "I'm so proud of you, princess. Just give me a minute though, as I have something to tell the IG."

He took Bhupinder aside and said, "Sir, I'm sure you have heard about the illegal poppy being grown at Jadeja farms."

The IG nodded. "I got your mail. But before I could take action, I found out about this man getting out of jail. Tch! So, what's the situation?"

"Sir, there are plans to set fire to the illegal crops. I'm off to stop that. It'd be great if you could send some backup forces to stop whatever's happening." He lowered his voice when the IG nodded. "And I don't want to take Yashodhara with me. Could you please…?"

"I'll personally escort the princess to the Thakore palace," Bhupinder promised.

Yashodhara had walked up to them and had heard everything even if they had lowered their voices. "I'm not a child. I can manage to get home by myself if you don't want me to accompany you." Sparks shot from her hazel green eyes as she glared at her husband.

"I know you aren't a child, princess." Indrajeet deliberately raked his eyes over her curves. "But right now, the area isn't safe for the Jadeja princess, with some of the farmers revolting against us."

"Will you be safe?" She looked at him, revealing her anxiety.

"You don't need to worry, princess. I'm ordering some troops to take over the area right now, before I take you home." Bhupinder reassured her.

"I'll be back before you miss me." Indrajeet promised, his coffee gaze clinging to her hazel green eyes.

He left with a wave, even as the IG made the call for the backup forces. "Let's go, princess. I'll get you home first. I'll take your leave, Rani Hyma Devi. I'm glad that Jaswantlal didn't create any problem."

Hyma Devi nodded her head, thanking the IG before hugging her daughter. She waved them off, planning to stay awake through the night, to be sure that everything was alright at the fields.

When her cell rang half an hour later, the Rani picked it up eagerly, hoping to hear good news. After all, the call was from her *munshi*. She turned pale when she heard what he had to say.

Prince Indrajeet Thakore had been kidnapped!

20

aja Gajendar Thakore looked up from the book he was reading, as he sat on a sofa in the main hall when he heard a noise at the door. "Yashodhara," he greeted his daughter-in-law.

"Hello Papa. Sorry I got delayed. But I went to the Jadeja palace first. This is Mr Bhupinder Sharma, the Inspector General Police. And Bhupinder Uncle, this is Indrajeet's father, Raja Gajendar Thakore."

Even as he shook the policeman's hand, greeting him, Gajendar eyed his daughter-in-law in astonishment. That was probably the first full sentence she had ever spoken to him. She was looking at him directly with eyes which were calm and steady. he was also delighted about her calling him 'papa'. He felt so touched.

"And how have you been, princess?" He enquired solicitously, after inviting the IG to sit down.

"I've never been better, Papa." Yashodhara gave her father-in-law a wide smile. "Where's everyone? Let me send a servant with some hot tea. I'm sure you'd like to have some, Bhupinder Uncle."

Bhupinder nodded, while Gajendar said, "You do that. You'll find our guest chatting with your Grandma. Ragini Devi has gone up to change."

Yashodhara nodded at him on her way to the *Rajmata's* chambers. Meeting Ramlal on her way, she requested him to serve tea to the guest. She walked over to Santhini Devi's quarters and knocked on the door, curious to meet Indrajeet's ex-flame. Would she be a fierce competition to her newfound happiness?

"Hello Grandma." Yashodhara walked in to greet Indrajeet's grandmother. "How have you been? You have a guest!" She stopped in her tracks, looking at the diminutive blonde who was comfortably ensconced on a sofa, her dainty legs crossed at her ankles as she sipped on white wine. The two women appeared cosy, and obviously they had been having a heart-to-heart chat.

"Hello, Yashodhara. Where's Indrajeet?" Santhini Devi looked behind her as if searching for her grandson.

"Jeet needed to go somewhere, Grandma. He dropped me off at the Jadeja palace and here I am."

"Come and sit with us. This charming lady is Juliana Davies. She's come all the way from the US, to holiday in Rajasthan. Ms Davies, this is Princess Yashodhara Jadeja Thakore, my grandson Indrajeet's wife." The *Rajmata* made the introductions.

"Hello, Ms Davies. Charmed to meet you. Welcome to our palace." Yashodhara shook the other woman's tiny hand, wondering furiously what Indrajeet had seen in the woman to have considered marrying her.

"A live princess. I'm truly amazed." Juliana's violet eyes glittered as she stared at the other woman's statuesque figure. So, her Indrajeet was married to this creature and they lived in this palace. She hadn't taken him seriously when he had told her that he was a prince and lived in a palace. If only she had realised it then, she would have been his wife instead of this... this large woman. She mentally turned her nose up at the princess even as she gave her a caricature of a smile.

"Some wine for you, child?" The *Rajmata* offered Yashodhara.

"Sure, Grandma. Let me help myself." She picked up the bottle of rosé wine and poured a small measure into the empty glass standing in the tray. She also topped the glasses of the other two before picking up her own, saying, "Cheers, Ms Davies. I hope you have a wonderful visit to our country."

"I'm sure. Thank you, princess. I think I'll call you that since I'm unable to wrap my tongue around your name." Juliana slid in the snide comment.

Yashodhara shrugged, sipping the chilled wine. She turned when from the corner of her eye she noticed her mother-in-law walking into the room. "Mama." She got up to hug Ragini Devi. "How have you been? Jeet needed to go somewhere urgent. He should be home soon." She was aware of how fond Ragini was of her firstborn.

"And you, Yasho? How are you?"

"I'm awesome, Mama. Never been better." She gave the other woman a wide smile. "Did you meet Bhupinder Uncle? He brought me home."

"Yes, I did. He just left, saying he had some urgent business to complete."

"Oh, he's left? Okay."

The four women sat around talking, the *Rajmata* steering the conversation. It was a while before Yashodhara got up. "I need to make a couple of calls, Grandma. Please excuse me. I'll wish you 'goodnight', Ms Davies. Mama, can you come with me, please?" She didn't want to leave Ragini Devi alone with the *Rajmata* and their guest.

Ragini got up immediately, a look of relief on her face as she exited the room and entered the hall with Yashodhara. "How did your treatment go, Yasho?" she asked softly.

"Perfectly, Mama. I'm completely healed. It was only today that the doctor pronounced me fit."

"I wish both of you could have stayed back and enjoyed a proper break."

Yashodhara grinned. "That was the original plan. Still, all is not lost. Jeet and I plan to go back once the farmers' unrest is settled."

"Now that's an idea I thoroughly approve off." The two women came to a halt when they saw Gajendar's ashen face as he held the phone to his ear. Yashodhara's father was stuttering on the line and looked like he might faint.

"Papa, is something wrong?" Yashodhara reached him first, taking his cold hand in hers to rub it firmly, trying to instil some warmth in it.

Ragini Devi joined her, taking his other hand. "What happened?"

"Indrajeet has been kidnapped." Gajendar's voice broke as his heart bled for his son.

"They are holding *Kunwarji* for a ransom." Kilachand sounded tearful on the phone. "What do I do, Rani*ji*? What if they kill him?"

That shook Hyma Devi up. Just when she was going to reassure the *munshi*, she recalled Bhupinder's words, just before he left with Yashodhara. "Don't trust anyone, Rani Hyma Devi. Not until the whole matter has been sorted. Anything you hear, call me or Prince Indrajeet."

"Alright, Kilachand. Let me see what can be done. What do they want?" She began thinking furiously. Why were they dealing with her through Kilachand Gupta?

"They want time, to save the crops. They can harvest the poppy latex in two weeks. If they aren't going to be allowed to do that, they want ten crores for Prince Indrajeet's head." His voice broke when he told her that.

"I see. And how much time do we have?"

"Two hours." Kilachand told her clearly. "And they insist that we should not go to the police."

"Of course. That'll be sheer insanity. We can't risk the prince's life. Alright, Kilachand, wait for my call."

Kilachand cut the call and turned towards Amarchand with a smile. "She'll pay. I'm sure of it. Where have you kept the prince?"

"I've left him in Meghnath's charge. The prince put up a lot of fight. Meghnath was the only one who could control him. But tell me, where will the old woman go for so much cash? And at such an unearthly hour?" Amarchand was worried.

"Perfect." Kilachand rubbed his hands with glee, thinking of the gigantic man in charge of the prince, before he said, "You don't know these royalty like I do. They keep a lot of cash stored at their residence. Moreover, it was only this morning I withdrew a large amount for making some payments." He had decided that he was going to keep the MLA out of the equation now. The man surely didn't deserve the lion's share in the ten crore rupees they would be getting for Indrajeet Thakore's life. Now they just had to wait and watch. They were still going to set fire to the fields once they received the ransom money.

One hour later, Indrajeet opened his eyes in a slit, trying to get a grip on his surroundings. He caught a movement in his peripheral and saw Meghnath move into his line of vision. "Don't you dare move. I have been ordered to shoot you if you try to escape." Meghnath threatened him in a hoarse voice. Indrajeet was tempted to laugh when he saw the comical expression on the bodyguard's face as he tried to look apologetic in the dim light of the lantern.

Indrajeet moaned as if in great pain. Someone had been lying in wait for him and hit him the moment he stepped out of his car. He had blacked out immediately. He wondered how long it must have been since they had brought him here. He saw two other men sitting closer to the entrance of the room, smoking. Looking up at Meghnath boldly, Indrajeet said, "Who are you? And what do you want? Are you aware that I am the Thakore prince? You'll be hung if you are caught."

He noticed the startled looks on the other men's faces from his peripheral. Good, his words had scared the men. By now, Indrajeet was aware that Kilachand had a major role to play in all this. He wondered if the police troops had arrived yet.

Meghnath replied, "I don't have to tell you anything. My order is to ensure that you don't get away from here."

"But why have you caught me? I am of no use to you. You people are really stupid. You should have caught Rani Hyma Devi. Now that would have made sense. No one is going to pay you one rupee for me."

"But you are a prince. Someone will pay a ransom for you, right?" One of the men at the door yelled at him.

Indrajeet laughed, shocking them. "I'm a prince who has a big palace, but no cash. What ransom can you expect for me?"

The door was opened wide and Kilachand walked in with Amarchand. "*Namaste Kunwar* Indrajeet Thakore!" The *munshi* greeted the prince respectfully.

"*Munshi* Kilachand Gupta! Am I glad to see you! Thank God you are here. These men are holding me hostage."

Kilachand laughed. "You are a fool, Prince Indrajeet Thakore. All these men are mine. I was the one who had you kidnapped. The Rani should be calling me any minute regarding the ransom money."

The next minute, the laughter froze on his face when he felt a large hand strangling him, as he was held up in the air, a foot above the ground. Meghnath was holding him as well as Amarchand by their throats.

The men at the door saw what was happening and ran for their lives, only to be caught by the policemen who had gathered outside. Four policemen walked in and handcuffed both Kilachand and Amarchand. Meghnath untied Indrajeet who grabbed his cell phone that was lying away from him and dialled his home.

Yashodhara picked up from the other side, saying, "Hello, who's this?" Her voice was trembling.

"Yash, Jeet here. I'm alright. The police have arrived and everything's under control."

"Jeet..." Yashodhara sagged on the sofa, tears rolling unchecked down her cheeks. She turned to inform her parents-in-law. "He's fine, Papa, Mama. Jeet's fine. Don't you dare do this to me ever again, Jeet. I might just kill you with my bare hands."

Indrajeet laughed. "I love you, my princess. Expect me in one hour."

"It won't be just me. Your Juliana is also waiting eagerly for your arrival. Let me give the phone to Papa." She handed the cordless phone to her father-in-law before hugging Ragini Devi, wiping away the older woman's tears. "Jeet's fine, Mama. He should be home soon."

Ragini Devi buried her face in her daughter-in-law's shoulder and wept unashamedly.

The *Rajmata* had heard the phone and stepped out of her room to find out what had happened, with Juliana following right behind. Ramlal was sent to make tea for everyone as they all decided to wait up for Indrajeet to return.

Yashodhara was far too restless to sit down. Was it only this afternoon when they made love for the first time? It seemed as if a couple of lifetimes had passed by. When she heard from her father-in-law that Indrajeet had been kidnapped, she very bravely retained her composure. It seemed as if Gajendar Thakore had aged twenty years in the one hour which had elapsed between Bhupinder's call informing them the prince had been kidnapped and Indrajeet's call to tell them he was safe. Ragini Devi had been shattered as she sat next to her husband, refusing to utter a word. It had been up to Yashodhara to keep their morale up while her heart was breaking little by little.

She would never let him out of her sight, Yashodhara swore to herself as she kept looking at the entrance, eagerly awaiting her husband's arrival.

And there he was! Her Indrajeet. His eyes devouring her, he greeted his grandmother first, touching her feet. "God bless you, my grandson. I am glad to see that you are fine."

"It was all thanks to Meghnath, Grandma. He saved my life."

Indrajeet hugged his father and mother. "It's so late. You people should go to bed."

Gajendar held his son in his arms for a couple of minutes, not uttering a word, before kissing him on his forehead. "Thank God you are safe, my son."

Ragini cried bitterly, her fist connecting with her son's muscular shoulder. "Don't you ever dare to give us such a fright, Indrajeet." Her voice was commanding, unlike her usual soft tone, making Indrajeet grin.

"I'm sorry Mama. Now cheer up. Aren't I here?!"

She smiled finally through her tears, letting go of him.

"Indrajeet!" Juliana greeted him, her voice a purr as she rolled her tongue over the syllables. "I see you are a true prince, what with the royal kidnapping and all." She threw her arms around his shoulders, going on tiptoe to press her lips to his. At least, she tried to, only that he turned his head away and she had to settle for his rough cheek.

"Welcome to my country, Juliana. Now, if you don't mind, I'm totally beat. I'll see you tomorrow."

He ignored her look of disappointment as he turned towards his wife last, his eyes clinging to hers. "Yash, can you please run me a bath? I feel battered." He threw an arm around her, uncaring of the rest of the family as he walked with her up the stairs towards their suite. He stopped as soon as the others were out of sight and drew her into his arms, kissing her deeply. "I love you, Yash."

She held his face between her palms, her eyes roving over his face. "Did they hurt you badly?"

"They hit me on my head." When she winced, he grinned. "Nothing unbearable. They had to get me unconscious in order to tie me up. Otherwise, it wouldn't have been possible."

"Very funny." She pushed him into the bedroom before walking into the en suite bathroom to run hot water in the marble bath. She walked out to see him pulling his shirt off. "Will you sit down and allow me to check your head?"

He sat on the dressing stool as she ran her fingers gently over his scalp and found a swelling at the back of his head. "Does it hurt?" She probed gently to make sure there was just a single wound.

"Not when you touch it, no." He pulled her on his lap, kissing the pulse at her neck.

"What happened?"

"Nothing much. *Munshi* Kilachand was at the bottom of it all." He paused when Yashodhara gasped. "Shocking, right? I didn't trust anyone and had Grandma's bodyguard Meghnath planted among the henchmen. It was quite easy after that. As you know, Bhupinder Sharma had ordered one hundred policemen to keep a watch on the farms. Meghnath met Bhajrang Varma, one of the good farmers, and instructed him to evacuate all the farmhouses in and around the area where the illegal poppy is grown. They were planning to set fire to the fields. I wanted Kilachand caught red-handed, and also Amarchand Khatri."

Yashodhara raised both hands and placed them one over the other on her mouth, her eyes having gone wide. "That Khatri, he was so nice to Mama when she visited his farm."

"Exactly. An MLA is also involved in this racket. But we have Kilachand. Bhupinder Sharma is planning to make him approver if he spills the beans on the politician. Anyway, it's all over now."

"What will happen to the poppy crop now?"

"We can sell it under government guidance and pay the appropriate taxes, and make the whole deal legal. It doesn't make sense to waste the crop since the latex would make for quality medicines."

She took his hand and they walked to the bathroom. "Will you join me?" Indrajeet looked avidly at his wife, desire burning in his eyes.

"Try and stop me." She pulled off her sari and the rest of her clothes in less than two minutes even as Indrajeet took of his pants and briefs. He stepped into the water and took his wife's hand as she joined him.

With a groan, Indrajeet sat back in the tub, pulled her into his arms, kissing her silky shoulder.

"Let's go back to Mumbai tomorrow." Indrajeet told his wife. He needed to have her alone and make love to her throughout the day and for several days.

"Maybe after two-three days, Jeet?" Yashodhara turned her head to look at him, kissing him on his chin.

"Why?" He growled, scowling at her.

"Your Papa and Mama were truly shaken today when they got to know you were kidnapped. I don't think we should leave them and go away immediately. Let's wait for a few days."

Indrajeet's brown eyes shimmered, his love for his wife increasing exponentially. "Thank you, Yash. I'm so glad you were there with my parents when they got news of my kidnapping."

"Shh." She pressed a hand against his masculine lips. "What's with the vote of thanks? They are my family too, aren't they?"

Silence reigned in the bathroom as they kissed each other for a long time.

"Juliana… what do you feel for her now that you met her?" Yashodhara towel dried his hair gently, careful of his wound.

He turned his head to bury it against her breasts. "Nothing."

"How is that even possible, Jeet? You must have felt something for her, right? You both must have had a physical relationship too." There was longing in Yashodhara's voice. If only she had known him for longer.

Indrajeet raised his face up to hers as she stood next to him. "I can't do anything about my past, Yash. Yes, I had a physical relationship with her. But I never loved her. I love you, and only you, my sweetheart."

Yashodhara looked into her husband's eyes and saw the honesty there. He had reassured her while in Mumbai too. But she had been startled when she noticed the avariciousness in the American woman's eyes. And hadn't liked the way she had thrown herself against Indrajeet when she met him today.

"Juliana thinks she has some proprietary rights towards you." It wasn't a question but a matter-of-fact declaration.

Indrajeet nodded. "Yeah, I noticed that too. You don't worry your pretty head about it. I'll send her packing tomorrow. She has no place in our home."

Satisfied with his answer, Yashodhara removed her bathrobe and took his hand, to walk towards their four-poster bed. Would he have the strength to make love to her? He looked beat.

"I want to love you. But you might have to help me along." There was laughter in his voice as he guided her hand to his crotch. "My body craves you, but I…"

"You lie back and tell me what to do." Yashodhara was an enthusiastic learner who drove her husband wild as she rode on him some time later, collapsing across his wide chest, as they touched the stars together.

"You are fantastic in bed, my princess." Indrajeet hugged her close to his heart, his lips on her forehead.

"So are you, my prince."

THE END

REFERENCES

1. Indian Royalty: https://www.scoopwhoop.com
2. Psychiatrists: http://www.illumeably.com
3. PTSD: http://web.wellness-institute.org
4. Hypnotherapy: https://www.dannapycher.com/

BIBLIOGRAPHY

1. *Many Lives, Many Masters* by Dr Brian I. Weiss

OTHER BOOKS
BY
SUNDARI VENKATRAMAN

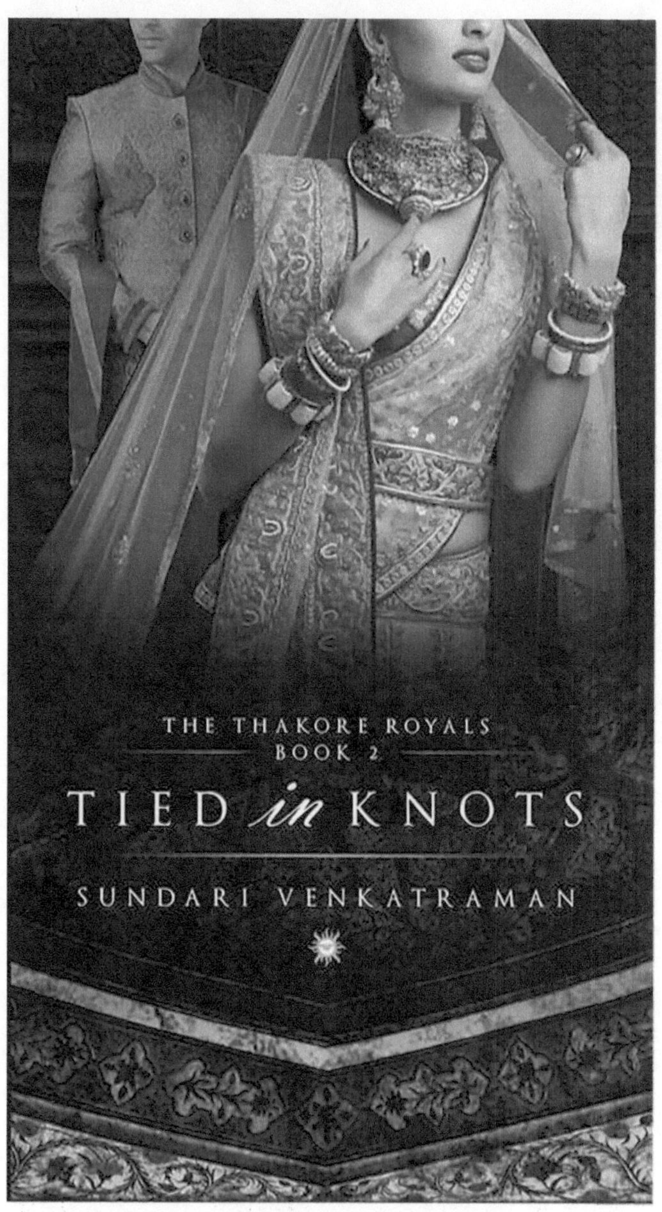
THE THAKORE ROYALS
BOOK 2
TIED in KNOTS
SUNDARI VENKATRAMAN

When Princess Chitrangada Vasudeva of Jodhana runs away from her bodyguards in the European city of Zurich, the last thing she expects is to be incarcerated with a stranger in his hotel suite for three days and nights.

Prince Rajvardhan Thakore of Udaipur is on his way to take part in the ice polo event at St. Moritz and plans to take a much-needed break in Zurich. He's thrown for a toss when he stops his car to help a damsel in distress. A few minutes into the encounter, he finds out that "Princess" is anything but a helpless female.

Sparks fly, and how!

Until that morning when Princess simply ups and leaves Rajvardhan without a contact number or a forwarding address. He doesn't even know her real name.

And then they meet again under the most unusual of circumstances back in Rajasthan, during Chitrangada's engagement to Raja Harischandra Gajanan of Indore. Even stranger is the fact that her fiancé is more her father's contemporary than hers.

Will the Thakore prince's endeavor to make the Vasudeva princess his own succeed under the circumstances?

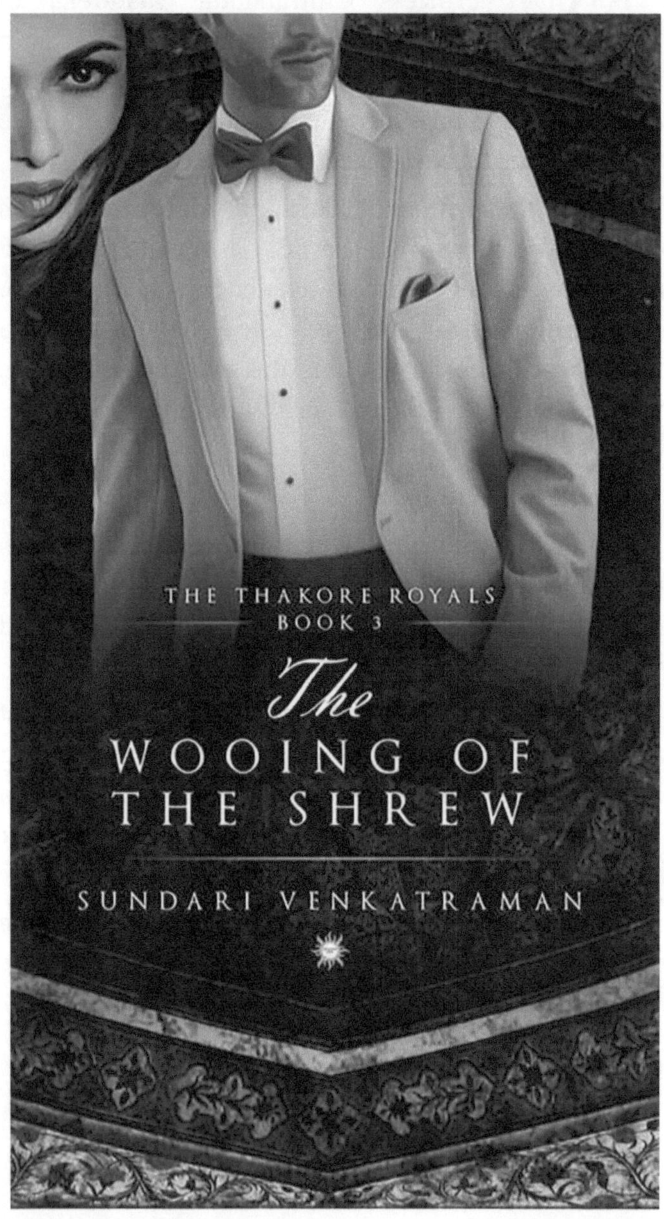

THE THAKORE ROYALS
BOOK 3
The
WOOING OF
THE SHREW
SUNDARI VENKATRAMAN

ayanita Thakore was a prickly princess who didn't care for the idea of any man getting close to her… until Prince Harshvardhan Singh Gaekwad turns up in her life.

Sparks fly even at their first meeting when the Princess of Udaipur clashes with the Prince of Baroda.

He falls in love with the fiery princess while she fights her attraction to him tooth and nail.

He woos her, beguiles her, cherishes her…

…while the princess feels that maybe he couldn't love such a tempestuous woman such as herself.

But before they could cross the great divide and get to know each other, something happens, something terrible that might just blow their lives apart.

Man Friday
SUNDARI VENKATRAMAN

Rituraj realises he's in love with the Gaekwad princess, Sitara Devi. The timing is slightly wrong though. Just ten minutes ago Sitara Devi married Harishchandra Gajanan. All of seventeen and nursing a badly bruised heart, Rituraj takes up boxing, hoping to build his strength and heal his wounded soul.

When destiny gives them a second chance, hope springs in his heart.

Rituraj grabs the opportunity of becoming Sitara's bodyguard-cum-assistant. He's the only man in her life but he's just her Man Friday. Since his father was merely an employee of Sitara's father, will he even be considered as a prospective life partner for the Gaekwad princess?

Sitara and Rituraj are crazily attracted to each other, yet they are unable to move forward. So where is the hitch? Why the fear in taking the relationship to the next level?

Class Barriers! Debauchery! Sexual Perversion!

It looks like 'Ne'er the twain shall meet'.

Read the book to find out if Sitara eventually gets together with her Man Friday.

Connect with Sundari Venkatraman here:

Sundari Venkatraman Books

Sundari Venkatraman Books

https://www.sundarivenkatraman.in

Author Sundari Venkatraman

@sundarivenkat

@sundarivenkatraman

sundarivenkat@gmail.com

www.ingramcontent.com/pod-product-compliance
Lightning Source LLC
Chambersburg PA
CBHW051145130726
47988CB00005B/2000